The Grumpy Dieter's Handbook

Produced by Salamander Books, 2013

First published in the United Kingdom in 2013 by
Portico Books
10 Southcombe Street
London
W14 0RA

An imprint of Anova Books Company Ltd

Cover concept: Frank Hopkinson
Cover illustration: Damien Weighill

ISBN 9781909396685

A CIP catalogue record for this book is available from the British
Library.

10 9 8 7 6 5 4 3 2 1

Printed and bound by CPI Group (UK) Ltd, Croydon, CR0 4YY

This book can be ordered direct from the publisher
at www.anovabooks.com

The Grumpy Dieter's Handbook

Ivor Grump

PORTICO

Contents

extreme diets, Homeopathic cheese pizza, Homeopathic light ale, Homeopathic café latte, Vimto Waft

Introduction

Diets are a bit like blogs, they're started with a rush of enthusiasm and the best of intentions and may turn out to be something that lasts a lifetime. Or, more likely, they get abandoned after a couple of weeks. The major difference between diets and blogs is that the Internet isn't littered with abandoned diets last updated in January 2010. That's because diets are tough things to stick to, but one diet has been more resilient than most.

The Grumpy Dieter's Handbook was written in response to the huge popularity of the 5:2 diet and its growing infiltration into society. There is a particular facet of the diet that turns normally cheerful, outgoing people into moody, food-obsessing, grumpy gits. It was ever thus with diets that limit calorie intake, but for these diets, people have assumed a continuous, seamless grump of deprivation over a number of weeks. Or, as we shall learn to call them, 'phases'. You know to steer clear of Mandy from management until she realises she isn't going to 'melt away her muffin top'. With the 5:2 it's not so clear-cut – normal eating is interspersed one day with very limited eating the next. It really is a case of feast and famine – one day going bananas, the next day hiding bananas.

Things could take a dramatic turn in the future with the 5:2 diet's widespread adoption. Local councils have already been tested on their readiness to cope with an attack of zombies and some have admitted that they have no contingency planning for such an event. But have they planned for an attack of Intermittent Fasters? They sit at their desks at four o'clock in the afternoon with the blood-sugar running low and the zombie eyes. The lights are still on but they're flickering. If a large percentage of council employees adopt the diet and choose the same fasting day, then it's going to be meltdown in the Parks and Amenities Department.

Not content with investigating the 5:2, this book also explores some of the other well-known diets that millions of people have been slavishly following for weeks, months and in some cases years. Some are sensible, some are extreme, while some are entertainingly barmy, such as the Fruitarian diet.

Fruitarians sound like kindly older folk who don't want to harm animals and so eat fruit instead. Like Rotarians but with fruit. However, if you adopt the fruitarian lifestyle you have to eat your fruit in a very particular way. Should a fruitarian catch you eating a lovely fresh fruit salad or maybe a bowl of summer fruits then they will zimmer over and steal it off you. Fruits have to be eaten one at a time, and with a gap of an hour in between each kind of fruit. It doesn't sound like the tropical paradise it's cracked up to be. Because of the low occurrence of protein in fruit you have to eat piles and piles of it. This overloads the pancreas, which has to generate a ton of insulin to get it all digested. The resultant health issues can be enormous.

One of the most recent trends in diets is to emphasize the kind of diet we had when we were running around speering woolly mammoths and gathering fruits, nuts and seeds. This, it's argued, has got to be a good idea because it's the diet we evolved from. Maybe it is a great diet for people up to 30 years of age, the average age at death of our ancestors, but what about the bit afterwards? And it's not really the diet they ate, because they ate the whole hog. You can hardly imagine stone-age man picking the crackling off a fire-roasted wild boar and going "I'd really love to, but that's going to play hell with my arteries."

We also take time out to look at that very private ceremony, when a dieter is alone with their scales and the moment of truth arrives. Has it worked or not? We take it for granted that we can weigh ourselves when we like, it's less about the opportunity and more about the psychology. In Lord Byron's day, the foppish dandies of the Romantic age, who were equally obsessed about their weight, used to turn up at their wine brokers who had a set of scales. Thus we know from the records they kept that the mad, bad and dangerous one's weight yo-yoed like Oprah Winfrey.

Weighing yourself after a week of dieting can be a bit like getting the bill at a restaurant; you have a good idea what it's going to be, but not exactly. And after you get the verdict of the scales there comes the whole trauma of 'why haven't I lost more?' or, as our cover suggests, 'why haven't I lost anything?' All that sacrifice needs to have an end result. But this book isn't about the pleasure of the success or the glow of the achievement, it's about the pain of the journey. Dieting is not easy. And you're about to find out many of the reasons why...

Ivor Grump

The 5:2 Diet

Old clothes reunited

The official Fast Diet, the 5:2, is one of the most innovative diets that has yet been devised. It's been gripping the nation ever since Dr Michael Mosley went on television and shared his thoughts about intermittent fasting (IF). Michael became smitten with the idea after the editor of the BBC's *Horizon* programme sent him off to do some investigation on the subject. The popular science programme showcased the findings of mainly American research bodies, who had run trials on fasting and its effects on weight, health and longevity.

Michael got thoroughly tested, weighed, wired up and analysed and then set off on his own journey of fasting for two days of the week to see what it would do to his body. For five days of the week he would eat normally and for the other two he would limit himself to just 600 calories. Instead of investing a great deal of time in careful food preparation and constant calorie monitoring he could eat what he usually did and then do the calorie calculations for just two days of the week.

After three months he'd lost 19lb, not a bad result, but you've got to think that having a BBC film crew following you around would be a good motivation to stick to any calorie-controlled diet over that time. Even those who embark on The Grumpy Diet™ might achieve that kind of result. But what staggered Michael (who comes in that great mould of genial, good-natured, TV-friendly experts occupied by *The Independent*'s Simon Calder and Radio 4 *Moneybox*'s Paul Lewis) and his GP wife Sarah was that all the other health boxes had been ticked. His cholesterol was low, his fasting glucose level was low and his IGF-1 levels (an indication of cancer risk) were low.

Apart from the success of getting a peachy set of data back and fitting into jackets he'd last shoved his arms down ten years ago, he said he felt fitter, more alert and what's more he hadn't developed a lifelong loathing of grapefruits. Having done it for three months, he was quite happy to continue for another three months had he been given the opportunity. That's the thing about the 5:2 diet – it's a bit like naturism – once you take the plunge and go for it, it becomes easier and easier. The worst bit is at the start. Or so the protagonists will have you believe.

Whereas conventional diets are at best a drudge, this is one where the dieters are happy to keep on going. So happy, it's almost like a cult. Judging by the footage available of most naturist resorts, it's a pity that these two don't go hand in hand.

Leave out the sea vegetables

Another added bonus is that it can be done on much less money (providing you ignore some of the authors' more Ocado-oriented recipes). Anyone who opts for the Macrobiotic diet and discovers the price of a shopping basket of organic food will know that their food principles come at a price. While it's good having the flexibility to eat local produce and organic fruit and veg that are in season, when 5–10% of your prescribed diet consists of sea vegetables, they're not that easy to get hold of. Sea vegetables are yet to become a dedicated counter at your local Morrisons or Tescos.

Diets regularly require lean meat, grass-fed meat, organic meat, lots of expensive out-of-season fruit, which rack up food miles, superfoods (such as blueberries) and very particular fats and oils. Then there are the food giants who have muscled in on the diet food business. It's no surprise that Heinz have bought WeightWatchers and that Kraft have invested in the South Beach Diet trademark so that they can give us carefully packaged low-calorie substitute meals as part of our calorie-controlled diet. There's money to be made out of dieters who want an easy solution.

Contrast this with the 5:2, where you can exist on lunches of Cup a Soups and carrot batons, knowing that tomorrow it will be bacon sandwiches and a Wispa. The added bonus is that food the day afterwards is supposed to taste even better than it did before, because you're getting back something you temporarily lost. A bit like make-up sex.

After the *Horizon* programme aired there was a torrent of interest in intermittent fasting and Michael hooked up with journalist Mimi Spencer who had previously written for many of the glossy women's monthlies and had already penned the book *101 Things To Do Before You Diet*. Together they wrote *The Fast Diet: The Simple Secret of Intermittent Fasting* – Michael went large on the science while Mimi tackled the practicalities and sprinkled in a few freshly chopped recipes.

Not quite as funny as The Fast Show

The Fast Diet is not meant to be a comedy book, but there are funny bits. It's so unashamedly middle class. Both authors assume that their readers lead very independent professional lives and are free spirits who can leave their workdesk at a moment's notice. Describing how he deals with hunger pangs late in the afternoon, Michael says he goes for a brief stroll until they pass. That's not so easy if the train you're driving happens to be in New Malden station. No matter how sympathetic they are to the drivers' long-term weight loss aspirations, passengers would probably sooner get home.

Actually, that would make for an interesting announcement from the guard. "Ladies and gentlemen, this is your guard speaking. The 17:05 from London Waterloo to Hampton Court is currently stopped while the driver takes a brief stroll to alleviate hunger pangs as part of his Fast Diet. Thank you for travelling on South West Trains."

When you think of it, there are many occupations where going off for a brief stroll might cause all kinds of complications. A bored City trader on the 5:2 might get a few tummy rumblings on a slow Friday afternoon. He takes Michael's advice and goes for a brief stroll – when he comes back he finds that the price of widgets has fallen through the floor on the Chicago Stock Exchange and that his bullish position on forward delivery has left the company staring at a $7m loss. "Thank you, 5:2!"

Having scolded other diets for piling on the complication, Michael and Mimi immediately let the side down at breakfast. After advising us to have eggs for breakfast they're keen for us to team this with smoked salmon. Another bit of champion advice is to swap out the toast soldiers from your boiled egg and replace them with asparagus spears. Get your butler to do this. Elsewhere there are terms that the committed foodie will probably take in their stride – when it comes to fennel 'it's great shaved' and to facilitate this 'invest in a mandolin'. Readers are also encouraged to *julienne* some carrots.

Presumably 'with a harpsichord' or other random julienning machine. Woosh. Straight over.

Another area for unintended hilarity is Mimi's obsession at getting Americanisms into the book. Mimi, da-a-a-a-a-a-a-arling, we don't add 'cream' to our coffee, we add milk. (The only people who add cream are restaurants who want to interest us in a floater.) We don't yearn for 'cookies' all afternoon, we long for biscuits. We don't have the 'get-go', we have the start. We don't get 'beat' we get cream-crackered. We don't have a 'cookie-cutter' solution, we have a one-size-fits-all solution. But best of all, she doesn't want us to gorge the day after a fast day… 'like a contestant in a blueberry pie contest'. My oh my, how many of those splendid events have I been to over the years in summer fêtes up and down the length of this sceptred isle…? None.

Your quick degree in biochemistry

To fully appreciate how potentially life-changing the 5:2 diet is you need a crash course in biochemistry. Those who follow The Path need to learn the vocabulary to converse with other members of the cult. This is what helps distinguish Intermittent Fasters from civilians. Most 5:2-ers speak fluent calorie and dieting acronyms. It's true to say that these terms are used across all diets and health programmes, but because the 5:2 is a far more self-controlled and self-designed approach you need to know what you're talking about. With many other diets the dieter simply follows the course they've been given with an aspiration that those who devised it knew what they were doing – but with 5:2 there are so many choices.

BMI – Body Mass Index, a pretty standard measurement and an easy one to check out. The BBC website has one where you enter your age, sex, height, weight and country. It then tells you if you are overweight, if you are above or below average for your country, and above or below average globally. It's the broadest of measures and doesn't take into account muscle mass – if you are short and very muscly, expect to be compared to a Fijian. If you are a short and muscly Fijian – no harm done.

GI and GL – GI is Glycemic Index and GL is Glycemic Load. The Glycemic Index is a measure of how quickly your body turns food, particularly carbohydrate, into blood sugar. The longer it takes, the more even the supply of sugar into the blood – which is good. It tends to make you less hungry. The amount of blood sugar is important because the more there is, the more your body produces insulin to cope with it. High levels of insulin encourage the body to store fat.

Glycemic Load gives you an indication of how much glucose is in the food per serving – so occasionally you get food that has a high GI but a low GL.

The brain ache part of these calculations comes when you throw in the calorie element, so you have to quantify the GI the GL and the kcal. Soya milk is low kcal but high GI. Dairy milk is high kcal but low GI – and what, we hear you say, about the LDLs and the HDLs of these two important dietary elements?

Oh, you're asleep.

LDL and HDL – This is a measure of cholesterol, which we all know about after decades of Flora adverts. LDL stands for low-density lipoprotein, which clags up your artery walls and HDL stands for high-density lipoprotein which un-clags it. So having low LDL is good and high HDL is good. If you're that way inclined you can express your ratio of LDL to HDL as a percentage. But we will make you wear a white coat.

LDL is also remarkably close to LiDL, where you can see many people with high levels of low-density protein struggling to get out of their car seats.

IGF-1 – This is a measure of cell turnover and hence cancer risk. Dr Michael Mosley says it's an expensive test and considering his fridge is routinely packed with smoked salmon and asparagus spears it must be very expensive. Nevertheless, when it's measured as part of clinical trials Intermittent Fasters benefit from a much improved figure. Ironically, those on a diet that recommends high quantities of animal protein can see their IGF-1 increase – so that's two fingers up to the late departed Dr Atkins (Michael and Mimi are too polite to say this).

BDNF – Brain Derived Neurotrophic Factor is a protein produced by the body. Fasting mice produce more of it when they're deprived of food and research suggests that it helps improve mood. This may account for the fact that after a few weeks of fasting in humans, the endurance of hunger becomes easier rather than harder. Certainly the mice involved in the clinical trial felt a lot more cheerful after a couple of weeks and whereas in the first two weeks they appeared tired and listless, by the end of the study they were putting on musicals.

The sum total of all intermittent fasting benefits are impressive. Even if your weight remains the same on the 5:2 you can look to a lower risk of cancer, a lower risk of a stroke or heart attack through a better LDL/HDL ratio, potentially a lower risk of dementia in later life, and some lovely kitchen accessories you'd never heard of before. What's not to like…?

The bipolar nature of a 5:2 dieter

One day they are spurning the offer of cake, the next day they are first in the queue. One day they are scrutinising the nutritional information on the back of a Jordan's crunch bar with all the reverence of a holy text and the next day they are barrelling into a finger of fudge without a second glance at the packet. One day they spend their lunch hour furtively looking for 150 kcal recipes, the next they are looking lasciviously at the Just Eat menu for the local kebab shop. This is the nature of the Intermittent Faster – they are two different people during the week.

Energy crash

One of the supreme tests of 5:2 dieters is keeping going through a fast day. While authors Michael and Mimi are very upbeat about Intermittent Fasters being energised by the process, the anecdotal evidence is that a lot of people feel exhausted. *Daily Telegraph* journalist Lucy Cavendish tried the diet but found it made her so weary, progressively more weary as the week ground on, that her children started trying to feed her, 'so that mummy wouldn't be so grumpy'.

This lack of energy is not surprising, given that all of a sudden you're subsisting on a quarter of your normal calories and your body isn't familiar with diving into your fat stores to provide energy. Suddenly denying it the usual supply of easy carbohydrates is a bit of a shocker. You can hear your body panicking – 'surely there's a local shop nearby? Use your eyes, any second now I'm going to start weakening your knees and then you're going to look stupid. Don't make me go into ketosis'.

All of a sudden it's like a Tour de France rider tackling the ascent of Les Deux Alpes, with the energy in their muscles as opposed to the glycogen supplied in energy gels, bars and drinks by the team support car. The top cycle riders like Chris Froome and Bradley Wiggins have to be so light on their bikes that they cannot afford to build hefty muscle – the energy is supplied en route.

Achieving the divine state of ketosis

This is the nirvana of all fasters and hardcore dieters. When glycogen stores are not available in the cells, the body resorts to fat (triacylglycerol) which metabolises into three fatty acid chains and one glycerol molecule in a process known as lipolysis. It may not be quite as good as glycogen – think of it like arabica and robusta coffee beans, you'd sooner have the much higher grade arabica, but if you're desperate for a coffee you'll settle for robusta. Most of the body is able to use fatty acids as a source of energy using a process called beta-oxidation. When an Intermittent Faster kicks this process into gear the body starts using fatty acids instead of glucose. But the brain cannot use long-chain fatty acids for energy and is reliant on a much smaller source of energy to keep going. Thus fasting, when it is at its most successful, is not powering our brain to anything like its capacity. This is the time we should be doing something that involves mild exercise but is essentially brainless. Like golf, or appearing on *Made in Chelsea*.

The 5:2 'Wall of Silence'

Using another professional cycling analogy, in the last fifteen years there has been a wall of silence about drug taking in that sport. There's that same wall of silence from committed 5:2 dieters – particularly from men who are intermittent fasting – not about being on the diet, but about how tired it makes them feel. When you're in the early stages of the diet it's fine to confess to a few doubts about how it's affecting you. The further you get into the programme, the more on-message you have to become.

There's a bit of macho pride involved, in that men don't readily like to admit to weaknesses. They don't cry, they don't get cold, they don't fear the dark and they're not afraid of spiders. They're not embarking on the SAS selection procedure here, it's only existing on 600 calories, and women are getting by on 500 calories. They can't admit it's tough because that'll make them look wimpy.

The second consideration is that people don't want to flag up to their employers that for two days of the week they might be working on three cylinders, not four. Your promotion chances won't be boosted if you admit that on two afternoons of the week you turn into Homer Simpson, so any questions about feeling tired on the 5:2 are instantly batted away. Tired? No. Weary? No. Exhausted? Sorry, dozed off there, what did you say...?

Mice make poor decisions on the 5:2

In laboratory experiments mice who were low on blood sugar and had been deprived food made poor decisions. Some failed to find their way back to the nest through a maze, while others dreamed up the idea for the HS2 high speed rail link. That's a joke, of course; the lack of glucose in our blood actually makes us focus more on short-term rewards not long-term infrastructure projects. It's when we have a lot of blood sugar available that we can burn up the cognitive energy and take the longer view.

Which would you go for – a small sum of money today or a slightly larger amount next month? A study in the American journal *Psychological Science* revealed that volunteers who were offered the choice varied depending on whether they had a high-glucose drink before being given the choice or a low-calorie soda. Those with a low-calorie diet drink chose the short-term reward; those on the high-energy drink chose the long-term solution.

The implication of this is that on days when people are fasting, their decision-making process might not be completely up to scratch. So apart from feeling lethargic and food obsessed, for two days of the week they might be lacking the blood sugar to make fully thought out decisions.

Politicians are a very image conscious breed and some will have turned to the 5:2 diet to make themselves more slimline and voter-friendly. This means that we could be subject to even more poorly thought out ideas from both sides of our government than we get already. There is a highly scrutinised register of interests in the House of Commons so that we all know which snouts are in which troughs. But surely we need to register our own interest at finding out which politicos are fasting, especially if they take red briefcases home and have a budget over £10 million to spend. On past evidence, Ministers of Defence in charge of purchasing have been on the 5:2 for the last 40 years.

Celebs and the 5:2

There was an article in the *Evening Standard* in 2013 which speculated about a number of male celebrities being on the 5:2 diet and concluded that men don't like to admit they're trying to lose weight. Celebrities don't like admitting they're on a diet for a lot of reasons. The main ones are:

a) They were never fat in the first place.

b) It forever links them with that diet. The Middleton family have made very few gaffes but the acknowledgment that they'd been using the Pierre Dukan diet before the royal wedding has linked them interminably to the French boulevardier (who whilst out on his boulevards collects things he finds and makes art out of them, which makes him considerably more interesting than Venice A. Fulton).

c) When they pudge up again, there's extra material to shove into the captions in *Now* magazine etc.

Obsessing about food

Something 5:2-ers will admit to is obsessing about food. On the days of deprivation and torpor, visions of fantastic meals loom onto their horizon, like a desert oasis. In their heads they cannot escape the song from the musical *Oliver…*

> Food glorious food – we're anxious to try it
> Three banquets a day – our favourite diet

Every so often 'researchers' come up with some spurious figure about how many times men think about sex. Sometimes it's 29 times a day, sometimes it's every 16 seconds. If you work as a literary agent it's an annual event. Whatever the true figure and whichever statistic you want to choose, the number of times a testosterone-fuelled male thinks about sex is nowhere near as much as an Intermittent Faster thinks about food. It's hard enough in the sterile environment of an office, but just imagine how hard it is at home, when you're surrounded by it – and shops are only a stroll away. It's enough to drive a person to live like a student – i.e. have a food cupboard that consists of a bottle of tomato ketchup and a half-eaten packet of cream crackers two months past their sell-by date.

Obsessing about food is bad enough but it isn't helped by work colleagues who change your screensaver from the Microsoft default to a fade-and-dissolve montage of barbecue favourites or images from the Austrian patisserie.

How to recognise a 5:2 dieter

• When you meet in the coffee area at work they give a short intake of breath when your finger hovers over the Mars Bar button on the vending machine.

• They say things like – "have you noticed how much the price of celery has gone up?"

• Soup has become their friend.

• They give a false kind of laugh when you say: "Did you watch *Master Chef* last night?"

• Midway through the afternoon you see them reaching surreptitiously into a bag of carrot batons and looking at them like they were fondant fancies.

• They look at what you're eating and immediately come up with a calorie total like they were *Star Trek*'s Mr. McCoy equipped with their very own calorie tricorder.

• They like a solitary lunch away from other people and their extravagant use of two whole teaspoons of vinaigrette.

• They don't think it's funny when you forward the Hotel Chocolat newsletter on a Monday.

• Salad leaves have become their friend.

• They take on the same kind of demeanour as your friends who are training hard for the London marathon.

• They have become short-sighted, having spent so long divining the calorie count on foodpacks which is always printed in miniscule type.

• If you bring in to the office a Multi Grande Starbucks Java Chip Frappuccino, approx 600 calories, and approach them with it, they will shrink away as though you were Van Helsing approaching Dracula with a cross and some garlic.

All you can't eat

One of the great things about the 5:2 diet and where it trumps all other diets, is that you can press the 'pause' button. Because of its great flexibility you can defer it for a day, or two days, or three days. Whilst almost all diets lock you into a programme, with a few 'treats' as a sop to wibbly human nature, the 5:2 has five get-out-of-jail-free cards. Weddings, celebrations, barbecues, parties are almost all weekend affairs and can be indulged without the "no, I couldn't possibly" excuse followed by the rehearsed explanation. "I'm on the Piscatorial Diet, this is my haddock day."

Along the same lines, Intermittent Fasters have nothing to fear from the all-you-can-eat buffet. Their only problem is all-inclusive holidays and cruises, where the food is relentless, 24/7, and the Fear Of Missing Out factor kicks in. Even if you aren't on the all-inclusive tariff, having adopted the careful eating habits of the 5:2, watching other people's wanton grazing might be a bit too much.

When looking out across the endless prairie of food that is assembled in some hotels the temptation is to think of what a buffet of 500- or 600-calorie dishes would look like instead: Individual slices of smoked salmon, two poached eggs on spinach, three grilled courgettes with half a tomato, half a pear with cottage cheese, rocket and tangerine salad, onion consommé, pineapple chunks. Actually, it's probably better not to think…

Things to avoid on a fasting day

- The boss.
- Crucial meetings.
- Getting into arguments.
- Making long-term irreversible decisions.
- Taking the kids anywhere.
- The kids.
- Going anywhere.
- Using a power drill.
- Installing complex software on your computer.
- The box of Krispy Kremes brought into work for someone's celebration.
- Punching the person who deliberately brought in a box of Krispy Kremes on a Monday knowing that it was your fast day.
- Punching them on Tuesday because you didn't have enough strength on Monday.

Great things to do on fasting days when you're not at work

• Inspect ceilings in your bedroom.
• Look up at the sky from your rear lawn – aren't clouds interesting?
• Recreate a role from a hit West End play; how about *Whose Life Is It Anyway*?
• Loll about and text people L.O.L.
• Test out all the chairs in your house – give them a comfort rating.
• Find out how comfortable the floors are, should you be inundated with a surprising number of overnight guests.
• Recreate a role from Dickens' last book, *The Mystery of Edwin Drood*. The bit where they go to an opium den.
• Have a two-hour bath and see how closely you can resemble a Chinese Shar Pei dog at the end of it.
• Read *Hunger* by Norwegian author Knut Hamsun (where he wanders round the streets hallucinating) and realise how much weirder this all could get.
• Recreate the role of Signora Madeline Neroni from Trollope's *Barchester Towers* – she doesn't get up much and holds court from a chaise longue.
• Learn to meditate.
• Learn thought transference.
• Recreate a scene from *I Claudius* – the feasting scenes where they lie around – but remember you can't actually have a feast, you need a lot of salad leaves.

• Pretend to be a student and that you are supposed to be at lectures. Then you won't feel any urgency at all to get up.

Enter the Valkyrie

A friend who had been successful on the 5:2 had a few weeks off for various reasons before returning to the intermittent fasting fold. She said that all of a sudden she noticed her mood swings on the diet. At the time, her daughter was coming home from nursery upset and Claire thought she wasn't being given the care and attention she deserved. Both parents went in to see the nursery when all of a sudden Claire found herself transforming into "Tiger Mom on steroids", tearing them off a strip and insisting things had to be changed and it wasn't good enough and generally wreaking fear at the sound of her – usually jolly nice – voice.

Afterwards her partner said to her quietly: "Think you might have gone a little over the top there…" Now when she goes to pick up her daughter there's a scramble among the staff to go and make coffee or clear up the soft play area or remove Playmobil from the drains.

So, apart from losing weight and improving lots of different health indices, the 5:2 can help you become more assertive.

Frequently Asked 5:2 Questions

Ask your grumpy buddy

Mimi and Michael recommend that Intermittent Fasters get themselves a Dieting Buddy when they start their diet so they can compare experiences and swap tips. Many partners decide that they'll lose weight together, which is the perfect buddy system. Even if one of the participants doesn't need to lose weight there are still a lot of compelling health reasons for having a go. For those who don't have an empathetic friend, let us provide answers to some of the questions that frequently arise. They may seem a little grumpy and short-tempered but we were doing it on a fasting day. We also ought to point out that they are given with only a casual understanding of what we are talking about...

Can I have sex while I'm fasting?

Yes. Most people find that eating and having sex at the same time is clumsy and can lead to confusion and awkwardness in the bedroom. Especially if you say things like, "I'd like a little nibble" halfway through. So yes, you can fast all the way through sex.

That reminds me, how many calories is...?

No, let's not go there.

Is sex any better after fasting, you know, like make-up sex?

No, because you have a basic lack of energy and it's all a bit of an effort. Many on the fasting diet have all the energy of a teenager asked to do a basic household chore, i.e. it's "eff-fort" just getting into a vertical position or breaking free from the tractor beam emitted from their mobile device.

I'm an American, can I also do the 5:2 diet?

No. Fasting is considered an un-American activity and may result in a visit from homeland security. Under the U.S. constitution citizens are obliged to visit a fast food outlet (ironically quite different from 'fast food') once every seven days and eat snacks at intervals of two hours or less. There is no 'small' in America, just 'regular', which is two sizes above small.

The only concession to reducing calories in the States is American milk, which is not milk at all, but the water collected from kindergarten painting classes – it's the water that children wash out their white paintbrushes in.

Are there gender differences between men and women?

Yes, we told you this before – women get 500 calories and men get 600. Though after intervention from the Equal Opportunities Commission, women will get 550 calories from 2015 and 600 from 2017.

With intermittent fasting there is obviously a hormonal dimension to be taken into consideration. Men now appear to have periods on at least eight days every month (or in the case of my accountant, 26 days of the month).

Should I play sport on a fast day?

Given that half the battle of a fast day is staving off the hunger pangs, then doing an activity that makes you even more hungry… well, you work it out Einstein.

What happens if I give in to temptation and have the odd rich tea biscuit or shortbread finger?

First try using the opening dialogue from Hugh Grant in *Four Weddings and a Funeral*. Because now you're going to suffer. Oh yes. Did you really think we were going to say, "ah get on with you now, it really doesn't matter"? You are so in trouble. You will now have to reduce your next fasting day to 300 calories. It's the fasting equivalent of 20 press-ups. Never. NEVER, let us catch you doing that again.

...but what if I did some extra aerobic activity to work it off, such as 70 kcal on the home treadmill?

You're like a great big kid, aren't you? What if I ate it standing on one leg and the wind was blowing? If we gave in to your pathetic appeal the next thing you're going to be saying is, "Can I have a whole Twix if I do a 170 kcal workout?" Get out of our sight, you make us sick.

Will I get headaches?

Yes. Probably. And so will the people who are close to you, plus those you meet on the daily commute and at work.

Is almond milk real, or do people put it on calorie counters for a bit of a laugh?!

Yes, it's entirely fictitious, as is barley butter and ant cheese. Come to think of it, insects are very high in protein and low in calories, but people would sooner be fat than eat them. Even the good-looking ones.

Are there any special groups who shouldn't fast?

Diabetics, children (even monumentally fat ones), sumo wrestlers and bus drivers. Comedians who rely on being fat for half of their act – such as Jo Brand. In fact, throw in men and she doesn't have much of an act at all.

What should I drink?

It's important not to get dehydrated so drinking lots of water, black tea or coffee is fine, or perhaps a fruit tea or a low-calorie drink. However, it is best not to be too hydrated if your fast day coincides with a long coach journey or any kind of travel by rail with a train company that has a poor record of toilet maintenance. Which is probably all of them.

Instead of eating a low-calorie meal could I use a meal replacement shake as advertised on TV?

No, buying a commercially available meal replacement shake from one of the weight loss companies is simply not middle class enough. Are these shakes readily available in Waitrose? There's your answer. Now you have embarked on the path of the 5:2 you must embrace all aspects of The Path. You must spurn normal fizzy water and only drink the Mimi-recommended San Pellegrino. With a twist of lime. Not lemon, lime.

Is veg the same number of calories cooked or eaten raw?

No, stupid, if you fry it there's bound to be more calories.

I've read that soup is a great appetite suppressant. Mimi and Michael say that a light broth or a 'kicky pho' is a great meal in itself.

Soup is good. Heat it up to the kind of temperature that could remove barnacles from old tugs and then you can only sip it gently for hours, filling you up slowly. As for the 'kicky pho' mentioned in the official 5:2 diet book, I'm afraid they're just winding you up. This is actually a service offered by Bangkok lady boys. These two mischievous rascals laugh every time one of their readers goes into a delicatessen and asks the person behind the counter for what is basically a topless… (well you don't really need to know the rest).

Can I really eat normally for the other five days?

How are we supposed to know the answer to that? It depends on how you hold your cutlery. If you hold your knife like a pen, then no, you can't eat normally. Similarly, if you hold your fork like a cowboy or the way a jazz drummer holds his drumsticks, no…

Can I make up my own recipes?

What, and jeopardise the massive 5:2 diet recipe book boom? Are you mad, crazy and dangerous? Making up your own recipes is a short-cut to a set of diseases last encountered by seventeenth-century sailors. You are not a nutritionist, you can't calculate the calories, and you don't know how to put together a load of pretentious ingredients. Let's be honest here, you wouldn't know the difference between an adorable miso and something a seagull dropped on you, so leave it to the professionals.

What's a realistic target to aim for?

Some people aim to lose a few kilograms, others slightly more. Unless you are a prop forward your target should always be that your thighs don't rub together alarmingly and that heading towards dry grassland in a nylon tracksuit, country park rangers don't rush towards you and urge you to go back because of the risk of starting a fire from the inevitable sparks.

Will the 5:2 diet speed up my metabolism?

No, but it does have the extraordinary quality of slowing down time on your fasting days. Watch that minute hand start to move as slowly as the hour hand...

Will it make me tired?

Some 5:2 dieters actually experience an increase in energy on their fast days. These are the ones who are on Ecstasy. Most calorie counters will give the calorific value of all kinds of herbs but they seem to omit Category A + B drugs. Which presumably means you can take as many Es as you like (always consult a doctor first). How about trying a poached egg on a bed of rocket, lightly sprinkled with Ecstasy. Not only will the day pass quickly, you probably won't remember how dreadful it was. Remember to take lots of water.

Can I add a third day if I'm enjoying it so much?

Yeah, right.

The Fast Diet in Literature

To fast or not to fast? That is the question

It's a pity that the 5:2 diet hasn't been in existence longer. It has become such a social meme you feel it would certainly have been included in the great works of literature had it been around in the time of Tolstoy and Ibsen. Instead of conjecturing how our essayists and novelists, our great social observers might have handled it, we've taken some of their best-known works and added an intermittent fasting dimension. Except in one of the quotes we haven't changed anything at all.

Pride and Prejudice, by Jane Austen

He sat down for a few moments, and then getting up, walked about the room. Elizabeth was surprised, but said not a word. After a silence of several minutes, Mr Darcy came towards her in an agitated manner, and thus began, "In vain have I struggled with a minestrone Cup a Soup with croutons. It will not do. My feelings for some serious carb loading will not be repressed. You must allow me to tell you how ardently I admire and love Jamie's Flavoursome Focaccia."

"I might as well enquire," replied she, "why, with so evident a design of offending and insulting me, you chose to tell me that you started the 5:2 against your will, against your reason, and even against your character? Was not this some excuse for incivility, if I was uncivil? But I have other provocations. You know I have. Do you think that any consideration would tempt me to accept the man, who has been the means of ruining, perhaps for ever, the happiness of a most beloved diet."

A Tale of Two Cities, by Charles Dickens

It was the best of times – five days of the week – it was the worst of times – the remaining two. It was the age of wisdom, it was the age of foolishness, it was the epoch of belief, it was the epoch of incredulity.

Jane Eyre, by Charlotte Brontë

"Do you think, because I am poor, obscure, plain, and little, I am soulless and heartless? You think wrong! — I have as much soul as you — and full as much heart! And if God had gifted me with some beauty and much wealth, I should have made it as hard for you to leave me, as it is now for me to leave you.

"Do you think I am an automaton? — a machine without feelings? and can bear to have my morsel of bread snatched from my lips, and my drop of living water dashed from my cup? Give me my wretched bowl of miso Mr Rochester and sod off. I'm going for a lie-down, me!"

Antony And Cleopatra, by William Shakespeare

"Eight wild-boars roasted whole at a breakfast, and
but twelve persons there; is this true?"
"Aye sir, his fast day was Wednesday."
    (Mecaenas to Domitius Enobarbus)

The Adventures of Huckleberry Finn, by Mark Twain

Some birds flew over just then. Jim said that meant it was
going to rain. He told me about all kinds of signs. He said
you shouldn't count the things you cook for dinner. That
would bring bad luck. He said it was bad luck to shake a
tablecloth after sundown. Seemed to me like all the signs
Jim knew brought bad luck. He said if you ate three
things starting with the letter 'c', like celery, carrots and
cheese that'd bring bad luck.
"What about cauliflower or cabbage?" I says. "They're
non-dairy and low GI an' all. Surely they ain't so bad?"
"Cauliflower is just cabbage with a college education,"
says Jim. And then we let it be.

The Diary of Samuel Pepys

June 6th, 1661: Up betimes and to my Lord Sandwich by 7 o'clock and then to Greenwich to Mrs Bagwell and did towse her. Dinner of a very fine carrotte and celery foup in the George, cold but very prettily done and but 120 of the king's calories.

June 16th, 1661: But thanks be to God, since my leaving drinking of wine, I do find myself much better and to mind my business better and to spend less money, and less time lost in idle company.

Treasure Island, by Robert Louis Stevenson

I remember him as if it were yesterday, as he came plodding to the inn door, his sea-chest following behind him in a hand-barrow — a tall, strong, heavy, nut-brown man, his tarry pigtail falling over the shoulder of his soiled blue coat, his hands ragged and scarred, with black, broken nails, and the sabre cut across one cheek, a dirty, livid white. I remember him looking round the cover and whistling to himself as he did so, and then breaking out in that old sea-song that he sang so often afterwards in the high, old tottering voice that seemed to have been tuned and broken at the capstan bars. Then he rapped on the door with a bit of stick like a handspike that he carried, and when my father appeared, called roughly for a glass of rum. This, when it was brought to him, he drank slowly, like a connoisseur, lingering on the taste and still looking about him at the cliffs and up at our signboard.

"Have ye got any kicky pho?" says he.

A Tale of Two Cities, by Charles Dickens

"It is a far, far better fast that I do, than I have ever done; it is a far, far better diet that I stick to, than I have ever known."

Are You a Hardcore 5:2 Faster?

Taking it to the minimum

Living on any kind of low-calorie diet isn't for the faint-hearted, and those who try the 5:2 and stick to it deserve our admiration for their discipline and resolve. It is a regime that appeals to the competitive side of human nature and helps distinguish Intermittent Fasters from mere civilians. It is the cult of 5:2. But whereas some followers adhere to Michael and Mimi's ground rules with a devotion that would make even One Direction fans look lightweight, others may bend the rules. Try our quiz to see how hardcore 5:2 you really are...

1. Someone at work who is also on the 5:2 diet can quote the calorific value of obscure exotic fruit. How do you feel about that?
a) Envious.
b) Not bothered one way or the other.
c) Get a life.

2. You always fast on Mondays and either Wednesday or Thursday – much to your surprise some friends invite you round for an impromptu barbecue on Monday evening. How do you react?
a) You say you can't go, it's your fast day (while secretly thinking, 'you must have known that, numpty!')
b) You go to the barbecue but drink sparkling water and eat only lean chicken drumsticks with all the skin and dressing carefully removed.
c) You immediately change your fast day to Tuesday.

3. There are many new 5:2 recipe books coming on to the market. How many do you own?
a) Four or more.
b) Two to three.
c) One.

4. When people notice that you've lost weight, what do you say to them?
a) I'm on the 5:2 diet – if you want to lose weight you really should try it.
b) I'm on the 5:2 diet.
c) Yes, I've been on a diet.

5. You're at a party with people you know reasonably well and one of the more outspoken guests is holding court and referring to intermittent fasting in withering tones, talking about a friend who tried the 5:2 but for whom it was a complete disaster – it gave them headaches etc. Then someone remembers that you are on the 5:2 and asks your opinion, so you are obliged to say something.

a) You say they probably weren't drinking enough water and hydrating properly.

b) You say it worked fine for you, but it affects different people different ways.

c) You say I'm not on the 5:2 any more.

6. In an uncharacteristic lapse of concentration you start to tuck into a Wagon Wheel or similar luxury biscuit on a fast day. What do you do?

a) That would never happen – you *never* forget that you're on a fast day.

b) You spit it out and bin it.

c) You keep going – calculate how many calories it was and if you can't adjust, you convert the day into a non-fasting day.

7. You're not the only one in your office on a 5:2 fasting regime, a colleague is too. But you can't fail to notice that on their 'fasting day' they have a bowl of cereal when they get in (which you clock at 175 calories), lunch of 200 calories, and a mid-afternoon snack that has got to be 100 calories. Basically, they're saying to all and sundry that they're on a fasting day yet you know from some simple calculation that they're not doing it properly. But do you say anything?

a) Yes, you tell them that they've got their figures wrong – they're not doing it right.

b) Yes, you go over and say, 'I don't know how you manage to cram so much in' in envious tones which will surely lead onto a discussion about the calories involved.

c) No – it's ultimately their loss.

8. When working out food for your fasting days you calculate the calorie count to…

a) Give or take two or three calories.

b) Give or take 10 or 15 calories.

c) Give or take 30 or 40 calories.

9. How do you think of Michael and Mimi, the originators of the 5:2 fasting diet?

a) Dieting superstars. If you met them you'd probably be a bit starry-eyed in their company.

b) Authors who produced a great book that you value highly.

c) With grudging admiration.

10. You have left your fast day to Friday, there's no chance to fast at the weekend, but you've forgotten that it's Sarah's leaving lunch at work. Working so close to Sarah you can't skip it, but these things are long rambling affairs that go on for two hours and then the bill is split equally. You can hardly eat anything given that it's a fast day, yet you object to paying a load of money for other people's food. However, you don't want to be the one that stands up in the restaurant and says; "well I only had the green salad…" What do you do?

a) Just as everybody's leaving to go you engineer 'an important phone call' so they all troop off without you. You join them as everyone's on their main course.

b) Have only one course but have the most expensive thing on the menu. Remember Lord Byron said that women should exist on a diet of champagne and lobster tails (see the Mad, Bad and Dangerous to Know Diet). If anybody raises an eyebrow say, "it IS my fasting day".

c) Only order a starter and hope people realise.

11. You're planning your summer holiday and the children (or your friends) are insisting you go to a big all-inclusive resort with fantastic facilities but where you'll be paying for a lot of food and drink that you won't want. What's your answer?

a) No – you wouldn't feel comfortable.

b) Maybe next year.

c) Oh, go on then.

12. When you hear someone else eulogising about the benefits of the 5:2 diet you want to…

a) Join in.

b) Listen to their experiences.

c) Tell them to shut up – it's not a religion.

13. It's Diet Wars! Somebody else says they tried the 5:2 but couldn't stick to it, however they've discovered the _____ Diet which is so much better. Like, so-o-o-o-o much better. Which of these are you most likely to say…?
a) "People often flip-flop around till they find something that matches their level of willpower."
b) "The 5:2 is tricky at first, but if you can get over the first few fast days you find it gets easier as you go along."
c) "Good for you."

14. Flicking through a calorie counter book you discover you've made a serious miscalculation on one of the foodstuffs and have been eating 100 calories in excess of your target. What do you do about it?
a) Take 100 calories off for the next few fast days to balance the books.
b) Make the adjustment going forward.
c) Nothing – if you were losing weight under the previous system then why worry. Measuring calories is a pretty imprecise science at the best of times.

15. Christmas Day falls on a Monday, with Boxing Day on the Tuesday – will you make either of those a fast day?
a) Yes, Boxing Day.
b) No, you'll give yourself a break till New Year.
c) No, you'll give yourself a break till January.

Score:
For a) 10 points, b) 5 points c) 0 points

If you scored:
125–150 You are so hardcore 5:2 you should work for the organisation. You have frightening levels of determination and are the most perfect evangelist for the cause – and defend the 5:2 whenever it is criticized, sometimes to the point of being downright rude. In fact Samuel L. Jackson's character in *Pulp Fiction* had a speech you might identify with: "The path of the righteous man is beset on all sides by the inequities of the selfish and the tyranny of evil men. Blessed is he who, in the name of charity and good will, shepherds the weak through the valley of the darkness." Ask your partner if this is you.

90–120 You take the 5:2 very seriously indeed, but there are still times (but not many) that you would prefer to oil the social wheels by keeping quiet about the virtues of your favourite weight loss regime. Given the chance you will gladly spread the word. You have an encyclopedic knowledge of calories and it doesn't take much encouragement for you to share that gift.

40–85 You firmly believe in the virtues of 5:2 and follow the rules as far as you can. There's the occasional bending of them to suit circumstances but no serious lapses. Occasionally you worry that you might be obsessing about food too much, and that you now look at food in a different way, but that's true of all 5:2 fasters. Certainly it will be difficult to push aside the knowledge that apples aren't as good for you as you thought they were.

10-35 You are committed to intermittent fasting, but it's something that has to fit into your life rather than you fit your life around the 5:2. You wouldn't suggest to other people that they should try the 5:2 unless they professed an interest in it.

0-5 You're not really on the 5:2 are you, but you can't resist a quiz.

That Scales Moment

The moment of reckoning

Whatever diet you may be on, whether a South Beach, a Dukan or the 5:2, there comes a time when you have to find out how successful you've been and face up to The Scales Moment. If it's early days in the diet and you've been good, then the chances are that you know this moment will be rewarding. It may not give you quite the result you were looking for, but the circumstantial evidence of slightly looser fitting clothes and your ring dropping into the sink will be a strong indication that the scales are going to deliver positive news.

Similarly, if you've been eating on the move, out to dinner at the weekend and generally overindulging, then you'll be pretty sure that the news is going to be bad, it's simply a question of how bad.

For the rest of the time – The Scales Moment is one where

the news could be good or the news could be bad, you can't be certain. It's like getting your exam results back week after week after week. You think you did well but there might be that question you completely messed up – that bar of Lindt white chocolate you saw winking at you when you were at the station and feeling like you needed a spike of energy to get home.

Timing

To be certain that you're looking at your lowest achievable weight, the best time to step on the scales is obviously first thing in the morning before breakfast. The likelihood is you won't have eaten for the last 12 hours and so after the morning ablutions, whip off the jim-jams and on you go. Except early in the morning (or midday if you're a student) is not the best time to receive bad news. Psychologically it's a bad time of the day to find out that your heroic sacrifice was all in vain and you haven't shifted the needle a millimetre.

What you should wear

The general view from dieting forums is that most people prefer to be naked when they step on the scales. This approach has drawbacks, particularly on scales in larger branches of Boots. What's more, it seems we're all

obsessed about eliminating any possible extra weight –
off come the watches, hair clips, earrings, bracelets,
murkin brooches, tongue studs, iPods etc. All this
ceremony means that the next time you weigh yourself
you're going to have to remove, uncouple and unscrew
these items all over again.

Preparation

Seeing as you've put so much effort into losing the
weight, the last thing you want is to squander it with a
pair of scales that aren't zeroed, so if they're the old-
fashioned needle type you need to be certain you're not
registering a couple of pounds before you even start.
Also, make sure that they are on a solid, level surface and
not wobbling about in the shagpile.

The majority of scales sold these days are digital and at
the fancy nancy end you can get ones that will give you
your body fat measurement too. The Omron BF508 with
its "8-sensor technology" promises to measure your body
fat and your visceral fat as well as delivering the gross
tonnage. This retails at about £50, but double that figure
and you can have the Tanita BC-1000 Body Composition
Monitor with Wireless Data Transmission, the Ferrari of
the bathroom-based data acquisition world. The term
'scales' is clearly not enough to describe the expanded
role of the Tanita Body Composition Monitor. It wants to

do so much more. As it is equipped with a wi-fi capability it presumably radios back to base what it has discovered when you step on its pressure sensitive pads and compiles a dossier behind your back about what a consistently depressing lump you are. Given my innate ability to press the wrong button on the laptop, were I to acquire one I would almost certainly link it accidentally to my Facebook page.

At the other end of the…erm…range you can pick up a set of Argos Value Scales for the amazing price of £3.56. They might not be as accurate as more expensive ones but they open up all kinds of décor possibilities. Most bathroom wall tiles cost more than this per meter squared, so if you want to create a really funky modernist bathroom you could cover one wall in 23cm x 23cm Argos Value Scales. You watch, some trendy home improvement show will be doing it soon…

Stepping on

It's the moment of truth. Drum roll. You step onto the scales. What is it going to say? On a modern scale the digits flicker, often going beyond the weight it settles for, then they calm down to deliver a less-heart-stopping verdict. At this point in time it has our total attention…which is always a selling opportunity. A friend whose husband attended WeightWatchers said that the route to the weigh-in was lined with a boulevard of treats: sticky toffee pudding but only 170 calories, Belgian white chocolate mousse at 100 calories a go. It was a bit like the childcatcher scene in *Chitty Chitty Bang Bang*, but for older people. And without the threat of incarceration at Baron Bomburst's castle.

Back to the scales, this would be the perfect time to imitate YouTube and flash up an advert before you get to the bit you really want to see. What better time to bombard us with low-calorie product adverts to take away some of the agonies of denial.

If it's bad news...

The needle settles, the digits stop, the weight is given. If it's much worse than you expected, then you immediately blame the scales. They're not working properly, they CANNOT BE SERIOUS! The barometric pressure has affected them. Water's affected their circuits. You knew you should have left them in the bedroom not the bathroom. They've never been the same since you weighed all the suitcases repeatedly before the Majorca flight. At the end of this tortuous process of more towels/less books/do we really need a hairdryer? the scales were so confused they wanted to give your suitcases their own Body Mass Index. The temptation is always to shoot the messenger.

If it's good news...

The scales are working fine.

If it's really good news...

Yes, that's what you secretly thought you were going to be but didn't really want to count your chickens. In fact, now that you've had such good news there's probably no need to weigh yourself again for at least a couple of weeks.

Old-school Diets

Our collection of old-school diets includes the F-Plan, the Atkins, the Scarsdale and the Cambridge. These are diets that have been incredibly popular in the past, but have mostly been relaunched or adapted to fit in with changes in the theory of nutrition. Also to fend off criticisms that they left you with the social acceptability of Johnny Fartpants and the halitosis of Walter the Warthog.

The Mad, Bad and Dangerous to Know Diet

Fad diets aren't a twentieth-century phenomenon. They've been around since Lord Byron's time. George Gordon Byron was the Oprah Winfrey of his age, a celebrity in the public eye who gained and lost weight on a regular basis. From records held by Berry Brothers and Rudd, a wine merchant in St James, London, Byron weighed 13st 12lb (88kg) in 1806. Bizarrely, the wine merchant was one of the few places in town where a Regency dandy could have himself weighed on a set of large hanging scales. They kept records of the fashion conscious young men, including Beau Brummel, who weighed himself there three times a year between 1815 and 1822. Following Byron's epic swim across the Hellespont in 1810 he had faded away to 9st (57kg) by his return to Berry Brothers in 1811.

In 1816, while Mary Shelley was writing *Frankenstein* at Byron's summer residence Villa Diodati on the shores of Lake Geneva, the Shelley's host was existing on very little. He would take a thin slice of bread and a cup of tea for breakfast, followed by a light vegetable luncheon and a cup of green tea when evening beckoned. He staved off hunger with typical Byronic excess, by smoking a large quantity of cigars.

Sublime tobacco! which from east to west
Cheers the tar's labor or the Turkman's rest.
Divine in hookas, glorious in a pipe
When tipp'd with amber, mellow, rich, and ripe;
Like other charmers, wooing the caress
More dazzlingly when daring in full dress;
Yet thy true lovers more admire by far
Thy naked beauties—give me a cigar!

Old-School Diets

Byron's Romantics strove to be pale, thin and interesting, causing a moral stir in the higher circles of Victorian society, similar to the argument about Size Zero models today. It didn't help that Byron himself had said "a woman should never be seen eating or drinking, unless it be lobster salad and champagne, the only truly feminine and becoming viands". There was an outcry that the nation's youth were starving themselves to fit in with the Romantic view of womanhood. Dr George Beard lambasted Byron's legacy with: "Fashion has joined hands with superstition, and through a fear of looking gross or unhealthy or of incurring the horror of the disciples of Lord Byron our young ladies live all their growing girlhood in semi-starvation, they become thin and poor, their nerves become painfully sensitive and when they marry they give birth to starvlings."

So, celebrity diets, yo-yo-ing celeb waistlines and the authorities worrying about teenage girls not eating enough for fashion's sake – we had it all two centuries ago.

The Dukan

Pierre Dukan is a former Paris GP who came up with a strategy for losing weight in 1975. Typical of the French, whose gift is to take simple things and make them more complicated, Pierre's diet has four phases and 100 allowed foods.

Phase one is the 'attack' phase with dieters aiming to shed a bundle of weight in a hurry by concentrating on 72 protein-rich foods. This supposedly kick-starts your metabolism and the target is to shift 2–3 kg in a week.

Phase two is the 'cruise' phase where dieters are sent on an expensive Mediterranean cruise and have to resist the enticing displays of limitless food 24 hours of the day. No, that's not Pierre's idea of the 'cruise' phase, his cruising involves adding 28 vegetables to the 72 protein-rich foods and letting dieters ease off, after the sprint start that was the attack phase.

Phase three is the 'consolidation' phase where dieters are shepherded back into the realms of normal eating and can say *bonjour encore* to things like *du pain* and *du fromage*. Plus for being bon dieteurs, you are allowed two celebratory meals, but go easy on the *frites* and mayonnaise.

Phase four is the 'stabilization' phase where dieters eat

pretty much what they like, but follow a few simple rules about protein and bran, and make a commitment to exercise.

One of the selling points of French diets is the supposed elegance and slimness of French women, who are said to maintain their shape well into middle age, despite being constantly tempted by chocolate croissants and their national obligation to buy a daily baguette. The explanation for this is simple. They all smoke like chimneys and French public transport is so rubbish that they have to walk everywhere. Our national girth is a tribute to the great British network of buses. And a few other things, obviously.

The Atkins Diet

Pierre Dukan may have been a bit of a svelte Parisian boulevardier when he devised his eponymous diet but Robert Atkins was a confirmed lardass. Atkins took the low-carbohydrate advice he discovered in a 1958 paper in the *Journal of the American Medical Association* to tackle his own weight problem. When that did the trick he wrote *Dr Atkins' Diet Revolution* in 1972.

The Atkins diet involved limiting consumption of carbohydrates so that the body switched to metabolizing stored fat. Dieters were free to eat any amount of protein, it was the carbohydrates you had to avoid. However, research showed that given such a tedious choice of foods, dieters simply ate less than they normally did. Nutritionists questioned Atkins' approach, particularly to the levels of fat he allowed in his diet and this wasn't helped when he suffered a cardiac arrest at the age of 71. The arguments still rage on about the dangers of excluding various food groups from any diet, but what Atkins helped to popularise more than anything else was the fact that it was the foodstuffs, not the calories that counted.

One of the reported drawbacks of the diet was that eating so much protein left you with the kind of breath which could lift newsprint off pages and needed an industrial strength tic-tac to disguise.

The F-Plan Diet

The F-Plan was THE diet of the 1980s – as much a part of our 80s heritage as chunky shoulder pads, ridiculous hair and Wham! It was devised by the founder of *Slimming* magazine Audrey Eyton and promoted the maximum intake of fibre-rich foods such as beans and lentils and more beans and more lentils.

It was a calorie-controlled diet, but with what – in the wake of 5:2 – we might now consider a very generous

1,500 calories a day to play with. That 1,500 was made up of more fibre-rich food than your system could cope with, but the good thing about that was that it made you feel full sooner, gave your intestines a good-old workout and was great news for your "gut flora", whatever that was. The great news for Britain's emerging comedy clubs such as Jongleurs, (which also opened its doors in 1983, the year the book hit the bestsellers list), was that the 'F' of F-plan had its side effects.

Was it the Fibre-Plan, the Flatulence-Plan or simply the Fart-Plan?

"Are you on the F-plan?" soon became a euphemism for, have you let one rip? That didn't stop its enormous popularity. In recent years it's been re-launched as the F2 Diet.

The Cambridge Diet

The early 1970s was a great time for glam-rock, miners' strikes and diets. We had the Atkins in 1972, the Dukan in 1975, but the one that really kicked it all off was the Cambridge Diet in 1970. Devised by Dr Alan Howard at Cambridge University, the Cambridge Diet was a very low-calorie diet, or if you like acronyms a VLCD. It was low in calories but high in its reference to Cambridge and Cambridgeness, wearing its academic provenance in its title. That's probably because it took its disciples down to 440 calories a day along with a whole bunch of vitamins and minerals to make sure your hair didn't fall out and your retina could still process light signals.

The diet formula was intended to fool the body into starvation so it burnt off all the fat, while receiving just enough nutrients to stop the body from devouring its own lean tissue.

It soon found a commercial partner and the Cambridge Diet lives on with its careful rationing of food over a carefully proscribed period. Like a lot of the diets that have followed, the 'heavy lifting' happens at the start, when for the first two weeks Cambridge Dieters only get liquid meals – shakes, soup and porridge. A bit like a diet enforced by old age and a lack of suitable gnashers. In week three you get the luxury of a nutrient bar. Wooh wooh!

It's an extreme diet based on meal replacement and it's no surprise that there is a range of products calculated to give you what you need and give the manufacturers what they crave – which is not a pallet of Belgian buns, surprisingly.

The Scarsdale Medical Diet

The Cambridge diet goes large on ketosis as do many of the low-calorie 'sprint' diets such as the Scarsdale, invented by Dr Herman Tarnower, in Scarsdale, New York. A sprint diet is where adherents go through a bit of calorie hell for some rapid weight loss then shout "bank!" and try and keep off all the kilograms they've shed. Ketosis is the process where the body switches to burning up stored fat when it can't find any carbohydrate in the system and Herman devised a strict 14-day programme that would get us all rapidly ketosing. That's provided we had a grapefruit in the morning to supply enzymes for us to ketose with.

Although technically all diets are 'medical' in that they alter the body's chemistry, the fact that Herman didn't come from Cambridge or Harvard or Yale probably necessitated the use of the word medical in the title of the book to give it a bit more gravitas. Scarsdale is about as big as Thetford in Norfolk and neither are associated with top-level medical research.

Interestingly, the devisers of diets may have their eye on the long view and a long and healthy life but Dr Robert Atkins slipped on ice and died from a serious head trauma at age 72. Two years after Dr Herman Tarnower published what would become 'the total plan for the diet that's taking America by storm' he was murdered by his long-time lover, a local boarding school headmistress. We are happy to report that Dr Alan Howard has suffered no such tragic end and in 1982 set up the Howard Foundation which has used earnings from the Cambridge Diet to fund biomedical research at Cambridge University, including three buildings at Downing College.

The Grapefruit Diet

There have been all kinds of grapefruit diets doing the rounds over the years. One used to be passed round as a chain letter. Another was a very low-calorie diet which amounted to little more than grapefruit and black coffee, plus a few elements of essential protein to keep the lights on.

Grapefruit is one of the few proven foods to do some good in the system, it has a low GL – much better than apples, bananas and oranges – provides dietary fibre and it also improves insulin response in overweight people. Scientists don't know why and it clearly irritates them. One of the claims for grapefruit (originally called a 'Shaddock' after the Englishman who brought the first plants to Barbados) was that it contained special fat-burning enzymes. That's not true, but it does help stave off hunger cravings.

In a 2004 survey 91 people took part in a 12-week study and were split into four groups. One group had a placebo capsule before meals, another group had a grapefruit capsule, the third group had grapefruit juice and the fourth group were given fresh grapefruit. At the end of the trial the people in the three groups that had received some form of grapefruit in their diet had enjoyed a "significantly greater" weight loss than the group that had received just the placebo. Those who were given the fresh grapefruit lost the most weight.

Grapefruit diets are generally a variety of low-carb diets where you eat half a grapefruit before each meal. Adding a whole tablespoon of sugar with the grapefruit isn't the best way to go. Not to mention the glacé cherry.

The Cabbage Soup Diet

Nobody could accuse promoters of the Cabbage Soup Diet of glamming it up or selling us an impossible dream. As an aspirational lifestyle choice the Cabbage Soup Diet is right up there with the Irritable Bowel Syndrome Diet. You can imagine a group of young mums discussing their diet choices over coffee:

"Chloe, are you on the Dukan?"
"No, I'm trying the Beverly Hills, what about you?"
"I'm six days into the South Beach diet. Carol you're on a diet aren't you…? Carol, you've gone very quiet."

It's not hard to guess what the central foodstuff in this diet is, but if you don't like cabbage, cheer up, the diet only lasts for seven days. As historic diets go it's probably the oldest still in use. Over the years it has appeared in many different forms – it's been called Doughboy Cabbage Soup and the WWI diet and later evolved into the TWA Stewardess Diet. Legend has it that American troops in France needed fresh vegetables in their diet to prevent the onset of scurvy, but as they got to Europe six months before the end of a hard-fought war, fruit and veg (and trees) were thin on the ground and all there was to eat was cabbage.

Over the years the recipe has been adapted with various additions and subtractions. It's not simply cabbage, water and salt and pepper to taste:

Cabbage soup ingredients:
6 large onions
2 green peppers
1 or 2 cans diced tomatoes
1 bunch of celery
1 sachet of dry onion soup mix
1 or 2 bouillon cubes
1 large cabbage

There's no mention of 'The Soup Stone' – as in the children's story where the soup stone goes into the pot first and villagers gradually bring out bits and pieces to add to the broth – but it's that kind of recipe. There are many variations, just as there are with soup stone soup; Military Cabbage Soup has two large cans of chicken broth added, while the Green Cabbage Soup Recipe has mushrooms and spinach, with oregano, garlic powder and dried basil to taste.

The Cabbage Soup Diet has tureens of cabbage soup at its core. To this the dieter can add drinks such as water, black coffee, herbal tea or cranberry juice. Apart from an unlimited amount of cabbage soup, dieters can occasionally have a baked potato to arrest the boredom, and they are also allowed varying quantities of fruit and veg, depending on which day of the diet it is. However it's on Day 4 of the diet when things go a bit mental with the instruction: "Eat at least three and as many as eight bananas, and drink an unlimited amount of skimmed milk." The object of this banana-geddon is to end all cravings for sweet things, though the most likely outcome is that it will end all desire to see another banana.

For those familiar with the F-Plan or a boarding school education there can be side effects to the Cabbage Soup Diet. One of the best American dieting websites lists the social risks of the Cabbage Soup Diet as "embarrassment related to the risk of passing gas in public". It's not a risk, it's a locked on inevitability. Now it's very rare that you can get away with a 'one-gun-salute' or 'blow the big brown horn', 'cut the cheese' or 'float an air biscuit' in a business situation without some kind of negative reaction. Unless you're the boss, in which case nothing will be said...

Unless you've set off the alarms.

Is Your Diet Working?

You know your diet is really working when...

• You discover bones in your bottom you last felt as a teenager.

• You start shouting abuse at the television whenever John Torode and Greg Wallace come on.

• The ice cream in the freezer passes its sell-by date.

• Even a half-price Special Offer box of Maltesers can't tempt you.

• You don't bother taking all your clothes off when you weigh yourself.

• You don't automatically suck your stomach in when you look at yourself in the mirror.

• A friend treats you to a 99 ice cream and you throw the flake away.

• People gasp when they see you and ask you what you're going to do with all that spare skin.

• You realise that you can fit into your old wardrobe – you always loved those Narnia stories.

• Men whistle at you as you walk down the street (and it's an uncomfortable feeling being whistled at by another man).

• All your rings end up in the sink.

• You stop lying about your waist size.

• When the pizza comes round you automatically reach for the smallest piece.

• You dream about mountains of radiccio and rocket smothered in low-calorie dressing.

• You look at garden rakes and think 'fat boy!'

You know your diet is NOT working when...

• You catch yourself describing Boris Johnson as waif-like.

• British Airways say they're sorry they can't accommodate you on their regular flights, have you tried cargo?

• It takes longer to get out of your car seat than its speed from 0-60mph.

• Your onesie becomes a tight-fitting catsuit.

• You calculate that your average daily calorie intake is only 2,200 – then someone points out that's just for elevenses.

• You walk into a lift on your own and immediately exceed its capacity.

• You tell friends that your favourite record is by Luciano Pavarotti – the one for eating tortelloni in a bow tie.

• Seismologists can tell you where you went on holiday.

• You wake up and your bed is unexpectedly downstairs.

• At the airport it's a struggle to get through those bollards they have installed to stop you taking trolleys up escalators.

• You don't bother dividing pizza into more than two halves.

• When Channel 4 have one of their usual gross-out documentaries about fat people, you always calculate how many stone you'd need to get there.

• The local swimming pool issue a tsunami alert when you walk in through the door.

• After you've placed your online order, Tesco Direct tell you they'll need to get a bigger van.

• Small planets get sucked into your gravitational pull.

More Recent Diets

The old saying about building a better mousetrap and the world beating a path to your door can definitely be applied to diets. There is an amazingly large constituency of people who are tempted to try something new and even though there are old faithfuls like the F-Plan, the Cambridge and the Atkins to fall back on, the lure of a 'great new diet' is always strong.

The Fruitarian Diet

The theory behind this diet is that once upon a time we were all fruitarians, gathering fruit from the trees, berries from the wild and nuts from the monkeys. Fruitarian devotees will try and link Leonardo da Vinci to the diet and will claim that Mahatma Gandhi experimented with fruitarianism for a few months before reverting to his more conventional vegetarianism.

Modified Fruitarians will eat 80% fruit, 10% protein and 10% fats – this is the 80/10/10 diet. Hardcore fruitarians will eat 100% fruit and nuts and skip the protein and fat supplements which are needed to maintain sanity and essential organs. However this is not necessarily a diet, it's a way of life. The American website Diet.com gravely informs us that: "being a fruitarian or vegetarian is often seen as both a social and political statement. This can sometimes lead to conflict with family, friends, and even society at large."

Or, they just like their fruit and veg. That Greg Wallace is a fruit and veg man through and through and you couldn't get a lovelier bloke – even if he is subjected to foie gras risotto with a barnacle jus and expected to smile. Anyway, having a limited choice, fruitarians have spent their time dividing up fruits and nuts into seven categories.

Acid fruits: Oranges, lemons, limes, pineapples, strawberries, pomegranates, kiwi fruit and cranberries.

Subacid fruits: Apples, cherries, raspberries, blackberries, blueberries, peaches, plums, pears, figs, apricots and mangos.

Sweet fruits: Bananas, grapes and melons.

Nuts: Pecans, almonds, pine nuts, chestnuts, Brazil nuts, cashews, walnuts, macadamias, pistachios, hazelnuts and beechnuts.

Seeds: Sunflower, sesame, squash, flax and pumpkin.

Dried fruits: Dates, figs, apricots, apples, raisins, cherries, prunes, bananas and cranberries.

Oily fruits: Avocados, coconuts and olives.

There are many risks involved with a fruitarian diet because you have to eat a wide variety and a huge quantity of fruit to get all the vitamins and protein your body requires. Fruit contains a lot of natural sugar and so your pancreas is obliged to produce a ton of insulin to cope with it all. So while it's nice that no animals are harmed as part of this diet, the food mileage involved in bringing the word's biggest fruit cocktail to your door will produce a carbon footprint as big as Jeremy Clarkson's.

Plus, you don't even get to eat it like you would a fruit cocktail or a fruits-of-the-forest dessert. The Fruitarian Foundation recommends waiting over an hour between fruit types. If a person is still hungry after eating one type of fruit, they should eat more of the same type of fruit until their hunger is satisfied. If they mix up their fruits, the feeling of fullness is slower to arrive. Hence the saying – he's a complete fruitarian case.

The VB6 Diet

The VB6 sounds like a complicated diet, most likely based around vitamins – B6 is an essential part of the vitamin B complex responsible for amino acid metabolism. Actually, it's a lot simpler than that: VB6 stands for 'Vegan Before 6 o'clock'.

From the time you get up till 6pm you're a vegan, shunning proper milk, wearing tofu sandals and fretting about the psychological trauma experienced by bees when they realise their honey's been taken from them (their life span in the summer is less than 50 days so actually the ones that went out there and got that honey don't give a toss).

At six o'clock the world turns and you can slip into your best leather shoes, swap the plastic belt for a leather one and don your favourite sheepskin coat. That's not a winning combination, so it's best not to go out dressed like this, just revel in the purgatory you're heading for should the vegan police arrive, followed closely by the fashion police.

So, through the days it's nuts and berries and grains and seeds – a lot of black coffee and soul searching. After six o'clock you can eat what you like.

Interestingly there are a lot of vegans who get upset by

this diet. They object to the fact that 'vegan' is used in such a casual way when really it's a thoughtful lifestyle choice and not something that's set aside by the clock on a daily basis. Vegetarians drift into veganism and out again, but this isn't flip-flop, this is channel hopping.

Extend the premise a bit further and maybe you could try the PB6 – that's a Pagan Before 6 o'clock. Through the day you're a regular multi-god worshipping pagan, practicing idolatry and acting in a typical pagan fashion. Then at six o'clock, you become a Christian and recognize one true god. Vegans think the VB6 diet should adopt a new name and become the Vegetarian, No-Dairy, No-Fish Before 6 o'clock – but that makes it the VNDNFB6 diet, which isn't quite so catchy.

The 'six o'clock' concept could be the coming thing in dieting distinction. We've had the Doctor-inspired diets of the 1970s, the Plans, the 12-, 13-, 14-, 15-Day Diets. We could soon be experiencing a rush of before or even after six o'clock diets. Somebody has already suggested a VA6 – Vegan After 6 o'clock, so that all the animal protein you consume in the day gets digested and used up. This could be followed by the NDB6 – No Dairy Before 6. Or how about limiting the daily intake of carbohydrate with a NCA6 – No Carbs After 6. Or for the early evening confectionary intolerant – the NA8B8 diet – No After Eights Before 8.

The Gluten Free Diet

If you are a coelacanth then you cannot eat a number of food grains that include a plant protein complex called gluten, which is found in wheat, barley and rye. That is because you are an ocean creature and wheat-based products are hard to come across in the ocean trenches of the Pacific and Atlantic. If you are a coeliac it's exactly the same routine, plus you generally have to avoid oatmeal, as the milling machinery used to process oats often contains traces of wheat or barley.

This lack of gluten in your diet means you cannot really enjoy BBC's *The Great British Bake Off* as it means no bread, no cakes, no biscuits, no pizza, no pasta etc. Or at least not the conventional form. Such has been the popularity of a gluten-free lifestyle as adopted by the never-knowingly-chubby Victoria Beckham, Novak Djokovic and Gwyneth Paltrow that you can now get all kinds of gluten-free substitutes. These are as much fun as alcohol-free lager or a decaffeinated espresso or a low-calorie dip.

The Paleo Diet

Think of the Paleo Diet as the caveman diet. It shares the same root as the word paleolithic – "palaios" meaning old and "lithos" meaning stone. Paleolithic man was the first to use stone tools both to hunt and to prepare food. Indeed it's a very small evolutionary step from a caveman hunched over a fire with his stone implements to *Saturday Kitchen* with James Martin.

The Paleo diet aims to mimic the kind of diet we used to have when we were roaming around in animal skins two million years ago, hunting and gathering.

There are seven fundamental characteristics:

High protein intake: Today an average Western diet comprises about 15% of the calories in protein. Our ancient ancestors used to turn their noses up at the potential consequences for their IGF-1 index and wolf down 20–35% protein, especially when the moose were migrating through.

Lower carbohydrate intake: Walter Raleigh had yet to visit the Americas and pick up the potato and so early man would get most of his carbohydrates from non-starchy fresh fruit and vegetables. Paleolithic man (although it was probably paleolithic woman that did all the deep thinking) was well aware of the low Glycemic

Index of these kind of foods. A low GI is given to food that is slow to be digested and absorbed and it helped keep yer average caveman on the tundra fuller for longer.

Moderate to higher fat intake: You wouldn't catch our ancient ancestors pulling the crackling off the pork and going "Hmm, I'd really like to, but that's a heart attack waiting to happen." Everything got eaten. Hugh Fearnley-Whittingstall would have been right at home making entrail burgers and thyroid kebabs to put on the barbecue. The Paleo emphasizes that you can eat higher levels of fat provided it's good fat, like monounsaturated fat and not the lardass trans fats.

Higher fibre intake: Consumers are often duped into thinking that whole grain this or whole grain that is full of fibre, when unprocessed fruit and veg contains eight times the amount of fibre. So ancient man could get along quite nicely with what he gathered before turning to agriculture culture.

More potassium, less sodium: There were far more important items to be crafted from stone than a cruet set and so ancient man was stuck with the salt he received through his food. In fruit and vegetables the ratio is far more potassium to sodium. Which is good, because high sodium and low potassium is the bane of urban man, causing high blood pressure, heart disease and strokes.

Less acid food: The net acidity of Stone-age man's diet created few ulcers.

Higher intake of vitamins, minerals and anti-oxidants: Following the rule that all the healthy stuff is usually in the skins you peel off.

So, the reason we survived as a race is that paleolithic man had a lot of great ideas when it came to a balanced diet. It would be churlish to point out at this stage that the average life expectancy of a caveman was about 30 and that they wouldn't even have lived long enough to be turfed out of Metropolis in *Logan's Run*.

When you apply these fundamentals to foods you are allowed to eat in the twenty-first century, the caveman lifestyle becomes less appealing:

Allowed: Fresh fruit and veg, eggs, nuts and seeds, a selection of oils such as olive, walnut and avocado, fish, seafood and naturally grazed meats such as beef, lamb, venison, goat, moose, buffalo, antelope, gazelle, zebra, and coypu (some of these we've added - can you tell?).

Not Allowed: Dairy, potatoes, cereal grains, refined sugar, salt, legumes and corn-fed meats.

As with most money-spinning diets you can buy a whole range of Paleo recipe books and menu plans. For the hardcore diet fan, who likes their diet to do what it says on the tin, they are very un-cavemanlike.

Breakfast: Grapefruit segments and herbal tea with free-range eggs scrambled in olive oil and chopped basil.
Lunch: Caesar salad with a little lemon dressing and sparkling mineral water.
Dinner: Lightly grilled chicken breast, steamed broccoli and artichokes, followed by a bowl of fresh blueberries and melon juice.

It's not exactly *One Million Years B.C.*, is it?

The Beverly Hills Diet

The Beverly Hills Diet was devised by Judy Mazel in 1981 and as with all successful diet books of the past there was a revised version, the *New Beverly Hills Diet* in 1996. Judy moved from Chicago to California to get work as an actress, but struggled to get into the profession and found it tough keeping her weight in check. She started writing dieting books based on her personal experiences, and claimed to have lost 30kg using her own diet.

The Beverly Hills Diet advocates that protein and carbohydrates can't be eaten together. So that's fish but no chips. Fat is allowed to be eaten with either group, but may not be eaten with fruit. Fruits are particularly stand-offish in this diet and get the Fruitarian approach, i.e. you can only eat fruit on its own, one fruit at a time, and you have to leave at least an hour before eating another kind of fruit. Fruit is always the first food of the day.

The original version of the Beverly Hills Diet was a bit hardcore when it came to its love of fruit, which was the only thing on the menu for the first 10 days. There were no cheeky little waffles with maple syrup as a reward for staring down all that pineapple and papaya. More importantly, the first 10 days gave dieters insignificant amounts of protein and so in the revised version the protein appears on Day 6. This lack of a balanced nutritional base for a number of days always worries the professionals, but not Arnie's ex Maria Shriver who is said to be a fan. That's one of the good things about living in California, there is a lot of exotic fruit around. Try doing it in the Moscow suburbs where seasonal fruit and vegetables all come from under the ground. That's why the best-selling Russian diet book of 2013 was Svetlana Pankatova's **Моя жизнь со свеклой** or *My Life With Beetroot*.

Judy Mazel died of peripheral vascular disease, at age 63, in 2007.

The Warrior Diet

This kind of diet really ought to appeal to the *Men's Health*-reading constituency, because it's got a big, tough, macho title. Its author, Ori Hofmekler, is the founder of Defense Nutrition, he is "a modern renaissance man whose formative military experience prompted a life interest in survival science." Ori is a former *Penthouse* magazine columnist and, like all Israelis, had to do his military service and it was while in the army that he first started thinking about what kind of eating patterns gave him the best mental clarity. Hofmekler noticed that during the days where he ate throughout the day he was less focused than the times where he was forced to skip meals.

Hofmekler is a fan of the intermittent fasting technique and urges people to eat little through the day, saving it all up for a big meal in the evening. This imitates both hunter-gatherers who were out hunter-gathering in the day and Roman soldiers who would be expected to stave off hunger during the day while there was a chance of combat and then eat a big meal in the evening when darkness closed in and the threat of fighting receded. He points out that the Greeks and Romans used to teach their children to go through hunger and it was something the Israeli army taught their soldiers to handle.

Along with the dietary constraints there is a system of

exercise that he has dubbed Controlled Fatigue Training (CFT), which requires people to exercise when they are already pretty knackered, using workouts that imitate the fight-or-flight responses that prehistoric man drew on when a nasty-looking mammoth or a sabre-toothed bear appeared around the corner.

This is all good testosterone-fuelled stuff for men who seemingly don't like to admit they're on a diet (especially the Lean and Clean bikini diets). But then we get to the small print. Ori is not a big fan of the hormone estrogen and there is a list of dos and don'ts:

Would-be warriors on the Warrior Diet must only drink filtered water, minimize alcohol consumption, eat only organic foods, avoid processed foods, eat carbohydrate last thing of all during the evening meal and minimize food that might contain estrogen; that includes limiting foods that are wrapped in plastic or come in plastic containers.

Now can you imagine some of our toughest warriors, the Parachute Regiment, foregoing alcohol, insisting on filtered water and eschewing plastic wrapping?

Thought not.

The South Beach Diet

Published in 2003, the *South Beach Diet* book by Dr Arthur Agatston spent over four years on the *New York Times* bestseller list and has sold in excess of 20 million copies worldwide, proving, if nothing else, that Americans have an insatiable appetite for diet books. Arthur's trade is cardiology and he's a bit of a heavyweight. Agatston was involved in important early work on quantifying calcium in the coronary arteries as a measure of arteriosclerosis (a preliminary condition leading to heart attack and stroke). As a result, when patients are screened for the degree of calcium in their blood vessels they are given a score on the Agatston Scale to gauge the severity of the disease.

The South Beach Diet wasn't intended as a weight-loss book, more as a guide to healthy eating and preventing heart attacks that was widely adopted as a good way to shed the pounds and kilos. Part of the reason for the book's success is that it didn't paint carbohydrates as the familiar villain of the piece. Instead, we were introduced to the "good carb" versus the "bad carb" principle. Carbohydrates with a low Glycemic Index that took a long time to be digested and absorbed into the bloodstream were good and didn't have to be ditched, while those with a high Glycemic Index, (high GI) were bad and should be avoided.

Not surprisingly, beer gets a bit of a kicking when it

comes to the Glycemic Index, something that the giant American brewer Anheuser-Busch disputed in 2004. When the South Beach Diet came out and roared to the top of the bestseller list everyone jumped on the good carb, bad carb bandwagon and beer was verboten. The company put out an indignant press release. "Beer, and especially light beer, is enjoyed responsibly by many adults who also happen to be on weight-loss diets of all kinds," said Douglas Muhleman, Anheuser-Busch vice president. "Beer has zero fat. Light beer is also low in carbs and low in calories."

The press release also claimed that beer was so low in carbs that the Glycemic Index 'could not be practically measured', according to research from the University of Sydney. Now we know that many Americans lack an irony filter, so there must be a slim chance they got hold of some Aussie student publication boasting the health qualities of the amber nectar and didn't realise it was an elaborate wind-up. This is not far removed from the Wikipedia entry for the South Beach Diet which claims Agatston to be a native of Zürich (he comes from Long Island) and that he allows dieters to drink unlimited amounts of beer during Oktoberfest (not actually held in Switzerland).

Like so many other diets, the South Beach Diet has three phases and Phase 1 doesn't pull any punches. For the first two weeks dieters are allowed no carbohydrates at all, whether good carb or bad carb, in an attempt to get rid of that pesky belly fat. Dieters can eat between 1,200 and 1,400 calories a day across three meals, but unlike so many other diets Arthur doesn't send the usual suspects, such as dairy and artificial sweeteners, entirely out into the boonies. You can eat low-fat cheese, lean meat, skinless chicken, seafood, tofu, eggs, a whole barrow load of veg and a limited amount of artificially sweetened products.

Did we fail to mention that food giant Kraft Foods got involved with the South Beach Diet when they heard the bookstore cash registers going ker-ching…? In 2004 they licensed the South Beach Diet trademark to produce a range of products that fitted in with the ethos and nutritional requirements of the South Beach Diet. You don't have to be George Smiley to work out that low-fat dairy and artificial sweeteners shunned by so many other diets gave Kraft a much wider product window.

In Phase 2 of the diet some good carbs make an appearance, such as wholegrain cereals, wholegrain pasta, along with nuts, beans, starchy veg and wine. Dieters stay at Phase 2 until they reach their target weight.

Phase 3 opens up the restrictions a little further, while still banning you from hanging around with bad carbs.

Critics of the diet – and it's a criticism aimed at almost

every diet, including the 'I'm Only Drinking ******* Water Diet' is that most of that weight loss is water. Well considering 80% of us is water, you want to say to these people, what were you expecting…?

The GI Diet

At first sight this looks like a U.S. Army-inspired diet – we've had the Bootcamp for the Beach approach to physical exercise where 'soldiers' are put through rigorous training to make themselves bikini beautiful. So the GI diet should make us like the ultimate GI Joe, courtesy of beans and standard rations eaten out of mess tins – right? No.

G.I. in this case doesn't stand for General Infantryman but the far more complex Glycemic Index. It was pioneered by Professor David Jenkins at the University of Toronto. The professor calculated the amount of time it took for the body to break down individual foods into energy that the body could burn in the form of glucose. The longer the body took, the better, because that left people feeling fuller for longer. Hence granary bread is much better than highly processed white bread because a lot more of it gets stuck in your teeth for later on. (And if you wanted to adopt the *Springwatch* approach to the – how shall we put it – output analysis, a lot of it doesn't get digested.)

It could easily be renamed the Traffic Light Diet as it groups foods into three different categories: Red – foods to avoid. Yellow – foods that can be enjoyed occasionally. Green – foods that can be eaten all the time.

And just like motorists approaching a set of traffic lights, you should never go through on red, you can maybe risk it on amber and on green it's pedal to the metal. The website for the GI book also promises a 'pantry guide', so if you live in the 1950s and still have one, then you'll be advised on how to stock it up.

Not surprisingly, the usual suspects of fruit, veg, fish and nuts are in the low GI columns whereas Rocky Road bites, caramel machiatos and pork scratchings (half your annual salt intake in one bag) are nowhere to be seen.

The Macrobiotic Diet

This is less of a prescribed diet and more of a dietary philosophy. It was first promoted in 1909 by Sagen Ishizuka, who you can find variously described as a "Japanese healer" and "Japanese military doctor". His belief was that a natural diet, where local foods are eaten in season, leads to a healthy lifestyle. The *shokuyo*, or food cure movement, also believed that it was the quality of the food that was more important than the quantity and that care must be taken to balance the yin foods with the yang foods, the potassium with the sodium, the alkaline with the acid food.

Ishizuka's work was taken up by George Ohsawa who attached the word macrobiotics to this food philosophy in his book *Zen Macrobiotics: The Art of Rejuvenation and Longevity* published in the mid-sixties. The traditional form of macrobiotics proposed that practitioners should move through a process of food elimination – gradually taking away all the different foods until the diet consisted of just brown rice and water. (Brown rice was considered to be the food in which yin and yang were closest to being in balance.) However, nutritionists pointed out the obvious flaw in this extreme dietary approach – not least the tendency of those on it to look like the cast of *The Bridge on the River Kwai* – and so some fleet-footed philosophical revisionism was needed to reinterpret what the master really meant to say about his vision for food and a long and healthy life. Without the appearance of death-inducing maladies.

The bad news for those wishing to follow George Ohsawa's macrobiotic path and who live in temperate climates is that exotic fruits are completely off the macrobiotic menu. Forget the bananas, pineapple and mango, the coconuts, avocado and tuna fish; all food must be grown (or caught) locally or come from a 400-mile radius. Imported food – i.e. everything you get in the Swedish Food section at IKEA including that stinky

stinky fish and Dime bars – is not allowed. Unless you live in Aberdeen or on the East Coast of Scotland, which (for comedy purposes) is just about 400 miles.

Other principles include:

* Eat only organic food.
* Use cast iron, stainless steel or clay pots to cook with
* Adjust "the energy of the food to the energy of the seasons and the time of day".
* Cook food over a flame but using liquids to boil and steam.
* Avoid dry cooking methods, such as baking and grilling.
* Meals should be planned to balance the yin and yang qualities of the food (see packet for details).

Essentially, macrobiotics is a local diet for local people that allows followers to eat what is fresh in season. It's very flexible and can be adjusted for age, gender and activity levels. It's also a rarity amongst diets in that it is a high carbohydrate, low protein diet. Over half of the food should be whole grains with about 20–30% fresh vegetables, 5–10% sea vegetables and about 10% beans, lentils, soy, fish and miso soup. It's largely vegetarian, although some fish and dairy products are allowed. The biggest problem for devotees of old-school Japanese macrobiotics is surely getting hold of the sea vegetables. It's not everywhere that stocks Arame, Dulse, Kombu,

Nori, Sea Palm, Wakame and Agar Agar. And there's got to be a lot of yinny sodium in all that crying out for some yangy balance.

George Ohsawa, the author of a health book and longevity guru, died in 1966, aged 73. Just sayin'.

The 'I'm A Celebrity Get Me Out Of Here' Diet

There is one diet that's always guaranteed to work and that's a stint on *I'm A Celebrity Get Me Out Of Here*. ITV's perennial favourite hosted by Ant and Dec has a ruthless way of slimming down the egos and the waistlines of B- and C-list 'personalities', actors, sportsmen and faded pop stars stranded in the Australian jungle.

Each day the public votes for the most hated or mentally-least-equipped person in camp to take part in a Bush Tucker Trial to earn meals for the rest of the group. The trials are devised to cause extreme distress and painful embarrassment to the participants, something the great British public thrives on. And knowing how tetchy the celebs back at camp will be when the trialist troops back with no meals and all the other 'celebs' have to give a grudging, "Oh, you did your best" only encourages the public to vote for that person again. As one Liberal

Democrat said after Conservative MP Nadine Dorries went on the programme, voting Conservative has never been so much fun.

Of course the celebs should all do what *Coronation Street*'s Helen Flanagan did one time, which was to give up after 10 seconds. Then you get the very clear panic from Ant and Dec because they haven't got their ritual humiliation on tape for the evening show and they'll have no hilarious moment to tease us with before the advertising break. People should do that more often.

When meals aren't won the unhappy campers gets a maintenance diet of rice and beans. In a particularly poor year for meal-winning TV chef Rosemary Shrager managed to lose 31lb during her stay, former Doctor Who Colin Baker visibly shrank before viewers' eyes and even the fit-as-a-butcher's-dog David Haye lost 13lb.

One or more of the more notorious trials is an eating challenge, where the celeb is given an array of technically edible inedible foods to eat, not all of them dead; things like a Kangaroo anus, fish eyes, crocodile penis, vomit fruits, cockroach, witchetty grubs etc. After a dozen series the capacity to introduce novel disgusting parts of Australia's national animal to munch on is wearing a bit thin, but it's still regarded as a staple of the show. It's even spawned a new online snack service. Now you too can eat horrible stuff like the *I'm A Celebrity* stars with the

Bush Tucker Party Pack. It's a bit similar to a KFC family bucket except it's filled with revulsion (and before you say it, no, not more KFC). Apparently there's a bush tucker pack to suit every pocket, but why not try the delicious starter pack of:

1 pack of toasted weaver Ants
1 Pack of Sago Worms
1 Pack of Bamboo Worms
1 Pack of Mole Crickets
1 Pack of Silkworm Pupae
1 Pack of Flying Grasshoppers

Compared to what the celebrities have to face up to, these are simply an *amuse-bouche*.

The *I'm A Celebrity* diet is always guaranteed to bring results. Nobody comes out of the jungle the same shape they went in – other than Ant and Dec.

Six Weeks to OMG

Yo girlfriend – get your skinny on! One of the most recent diet sensations is *Six Weeks to OMG* by 'Venice A. Fulton' who strenuously denies – fo' sho' – that his book is aimed at teenage girls (despite calling his book: *Get Skinnier Than All Your Friends*). *Six Weeks to OMG* is quite a different approach to my teenage sons who adhere to the

'Six Seconds to Om Nom Nom Nom' diet – they can find any source of easy carbohydrate in the house with the accuracy of a heat-seeking missile, no matter where you hide it.

'Venice' is actually a personal trainer called Paul – fo' sho' – and has done a bit of acting, including playing a Death Eater in one of the Harry Potter films. In his book he advises dieters not to tell their parents they're dieting in case it worries them. In the author's case that would need the services of a trained medium and a re-assessment on his views of the after-life.

Other Diet Books Are Available

It hasn't escaped the publishing industry's notice that there's quite a few bob to be made out of the diet book. Although basic dieting advice can be summarised on the side of a mug – Eat Less, Move More – many involve complicated plans and phases which need a considerable number of chapters to explain. The kinds of diet book on the market can be split into a number of different types.

The TV Celeb's Diet

Hairy Dieters Eat For Life
Usually, celebrity diets are promoted by beautiful ectomorphs from the world of film or television who trade on their glamour and loveliness. So it's great that

the Hairy Bikers, Simon "Si" King (he even put his first name on a character-controlled diet) and Dave Myers should have their own successful diet book, not least because they still look like they've got some way to go. And you can hardly be accused of glamming up the diet book business or selling an unattainable lifestyle when you look like you've dragged most of your outfits from a Humana clothes bin and topped it off with a few Matalan essentials.

When I first saw the biking cookery duo on television, dressed in biker leathers and travelling from food location to food location by motorbike I thought, 'hey up, the two fat ladies have let themselves go'. Now Si and Dave are close on becoming a national institution. Oh, and if you liked the book and want to combine it with some exercise, don't forget to place an order for the *Hairy Bikers' Fat Blaster Workout* DVD.

The Catchy Title Diet

Low Carb, No Carb, Go Carb
Some of the catchiest diets rhyme and this one's no exception. Generally speaking, everyone's got it in for carbs when it comes to diet books, so feel free to stick the boot in the title.

Carb Trouble, Oh Yeah
Adam Ant reprises his early hit single with a diet book aimed at banishing those troublesome foodstuffs. You have to stand and deliver up all your carbs – it's your money or your life expectancy.

The Specific Time Frame Diet

The 14-Day Diet
The 15-Day Diet
The 16-Day Diet
The 17-Day Diet
The Three Week Diet
The Four Week Diet
The Five Week Diet
Everyone likes a bit of closure when they're attempting a diet (that's one of the good aspects of Michael and Mimi's 5:2 Fasting Diet). The most important thing for aspiring diet authors is to pick a time-slot that hasn't been bagged already. So if you do suddenly hit on a fantastic scheme to lose weight, make sure it's within a time period that nobody's thought of.

The Impossibly Small Time Frame Diet

The 60-Minute Diet
The 15-Second Diet
The Nanosecond Diet

These grab attention with their brevity, especially with those complete slackers whose willpower lasts about as long as their goldfish's memories. In effect the diet advice being given relates to something that needs to be repeated over and over, or a piece of information that takes 15 seconds to take in. About the same length of time as an éclair.

The Sex Appeal Diet

The Flat Tummy For Women Who've Obviously Never Had Children Diet

This diet is only intended for women who live near palm trees, preferably with a sloping trunk, and who like to relax backwards onto them wearing a CopaCobana bikini – or something not so dressy.

The Sexy Italian Chef With Lovely Eyes Diet

This diet doesn't work without the cover photo. The sexy Italian chef stares out at you with all the flair and humour of *Strictly*'s Bruno Tonioli but with a bit more testosterone and heterosexuality thrown in. Tends to appeal to women more than men.

The Green and Lean Diet

There is a series of diet books from the States marketed under the banner 'Clean and Lean' featuring a woman in the smallest of white bikinis, suggesting that you too could have a body like this if you got with the programme. 'Clean' is obviously a feelgood positive word and in the best tradition of rhyming titles goes pretty well with 'lean'. But if you think about it for more than eight seconds, which diet isn't clean? You don't have The Clean 5:2 Fasting Diet (thought to be such an improvement on The Dirty 5:2).

There are so many more words which rhyme with 'lean' that could extend the franchise. How about The Green and Lean Diet featuring an attractive dreadlocked slender vegan in an eco-friendly, knitted hessian bikini. Lounging against a recycling centre bin.

Or how about the Mean and Lean diet. It's the same set of recipes as the Clean and Lean diet, you just shout at your food before you eat it. That stress release will surely ramp up the metabolism and help kill the carbs.

Or maybe combine all of them to have the Clean, Lean, Mean and Green Diet Machine.

The Novelty Diet

The "I Can't Believe It's A Diet" Diet

For this diet you are hoodwinked into leaving out one or two bizarre ingredients from your normal roster of foods and it supposedly counts as a diet. The trick with these kind of diets is that it all seems very easy. You get the validation and the reassurance that you are on a proper diet (because it says Diet on the front, and, it's endorsed by an ageing C-list celebrity) yet you don't have to change your eating habits too much. And those extra kilograms you've always wanted to shift – they'll be with you for the long haul.

Grumpy Diets

Anyone can do it

It's fair to say that the Hairy Bikers know quite a bit about food and losing weight, and hence are perfect authors for a book on dieting. But it's a field that's occupied by many people who are far less qualified, who have tried their own unique method of losing weight, found that it works and then written a book to share their experiences. Quite often they can get the idea across in a couple of pages and so there's a lot of padding goes on after that. Robert Cameron, who wrote *The Drinking Man's Diet* in 1964 felt he'd said enough in 48 pages and left it at that. Cameron was an interesting guy, a photographer who published many large format aerial photography books on American cities and unlike so many diet gurus lived to the ripe old age of 98.

To give you an idea of how easy it is to think of a diet or a diet book, we've compiled our own series of grumpy diets. These are not medically approved diets and are – as the warning signs often say – for demonstration purposes only. Although none are so stupid as the Breatharian diet, which should have it's own special category of stupid, way beyond anything we could dream up. BTW, if any of them are taken, padded out and become international bestsellers, we thought of them first.

The Frank McCourt Diet*
Go to bed hungry

The essence of this Pulitzer Prize-winning diet is, as the line above says, to go to bed hungry. What's the point in eating a stack of carbohydrates then going to bed and letting your body stash it away in the love handles area. You're not a Sumo wrestler. The earlier you eat in the evening the more chance you've got to burn off the calories of the evening meal. You just need to pace yourself so that the arms of Morpheus descend just as you're beginning to feel hungry. Like young Frank.

*Frank McCourt is the Irish author of *Angela's Ashes*, in which he depicts growing up in abject poverty in Limerick with an alcoholic father who rarely took money home and then abandons his wife and family. It helped coin the phrase "poverty porn". Although, after the book was published his relations, including his mother, disputed the degree of poverty he described.

The Mildly Self-Harming Diet
Thith oneth in very poor tathte

We're not talking major injury here, no, but some people are prepared to have their jaws wired shut or their stomachs stapled in a desperate attempt to lose weight. This is a much more low-tech solution. Drink some very hot tea. And we mean VERY hot. What happens? Your tongue – ethpethially the tip of your tongue – gothe all numb and it's really painful eating or drinking anything elthe for a good few hours.

Doing this conthithtently may result in you permanently losing your sense of taste, so do see your doctor before embarking on it.

The Father Ted Tribute Diet
"Down with this sort of thing"
"Careful now"

The third episode of *Father Ted* featured a visit from Bishop Brennan who wants Ted and Dougal to protest about the screening of a blasphemous film at the local cinema – *The Feast of St. Tibulus*. Ted and Dougal aren't that keen on the idea of any kind of conflict and make a half-hearted attempt with their placards that read: "Down with this sort of thing" and "Careful now".

This approach can be used for dieting.

Down with this sort of thing: Cut the carbs entirely; no potatoes, no bread and no potato waffles, which is an item that lives vicariously in both categories at the same time.

Careful now: Go easy on the dairy produce.

The Ben Gunn Diet
"I'd like a nice bit o' cheese."

In *Treasure Island*, by Robert Louis Stevenson, Ben Gunn is marooned by his disgruntled crewmates on the island because he lost the map and couldn't find Captain Flint's horde of buried treasure. So he has to exist for three years on a diet of fish, more fish, even more fish, seafood and coconuts. It's like a Hawaiian-themed Rick Stein diet. Gunn fails to realise how rich he is in Omega 3 oils and when Jim Hawkins comes along all he wants is a nice bit of cheese.

This is a fish diet – no dairy. It's no surprise that so many more people in Japan live to over 100 years than in any other country in the world (34 per 100,000 people), living as they do on a fish and rice diet. The secret of longevity is to persecute wales.

The Student Diet
Life is a pot noodle

Give yourself £7.48 to live on for a whole week. That automatically cuts out the red meat from the shopping list… and you can probably put away the sea bass and monkfish recipes while you're at it. With the average daily intake of 2,500 calories for men and 2,000 for women, it's unlikely you can afford between 14,000 and 17,500 calories of anything over a week. Even coal. So it's an enforced diet, in which you'll get to know the major supermarkets' value ranges in great detail.

The Cross-Channel Ferries Diet
Getting to France fast

This is a short-term variant of the Student Diet. What you need to do is pick a long ferry crossing. Maybe not too long, such as the 24-hour Portsmouth to Bilbao route, as by the end of that journey without food you'll be pecking at the bins like a seagull.

The Brittany Ferries-operated Portsmouth to St Malo route is a good one. Once you've locked your car on the car deck, and deliberately left all your money inside, walk upstairs. Once the ferry is underway you cannot go back to your vehicle until it docks again ten hours later. You have to survive on whatever you have with you. In the author's case, this has been done by mistake. Modern ships are very stable, but when the weather is rough in winter you might even feel a touch of seasickness, which can only help.

The Tramp's Diet
Plundering the hedge fund

This is basically a hedgerow diet, where you only eat what you can find on the land. There is an abundance of free food you can glean from fields and hedgerows – nuts, fruits, berries, mushrooms, leaves, bark, moss. Just look at survival expert Ray Mears. He's not a small lad by any stretch of the imagination and it's all thanks to nature's larder, which Ray regularly plunders.

While you might gaze out on what you think is a boggy wasteland, Ray's eyes have already lit up at the prospect of a healthy and nutritious dinner. He'll be totting up the ingredient list like it was an episode of *Ready Steady Cook*.

Using a variety of traps and snares made entirely from willow twigs and gorse, Ray can also trap rabbits, trout, pheasant, partridge, wood pigeon and duck to provide a sumptuous meal fit for any king of the road. Although the cutlery might not be up to all that – unless you like eating with willow.

The Urban Tramp's Diet
Becoming Forage Grump

This is a variation of the rural tramp's diet but foraging is limited to urban areas. There is more competition for resources in the city so you need to adopt a combative demeanour. One of the best sources of food is normally a bin next to a bench about 200 yards from a take-away.

The Boots Three-For-Two Diet
Cutting out 33%

Based on that solid principle introduced by Boots all those years ago in a Christmas promotion. You buy three Xmas gifts and you get the cheapest one free. The same concept can be applied to dieting. Look at the three most calorific things you like to eat. But instead of getting the cheapest for free, you cut out the most expensive item in calorific terms from your diet.

The PhotoShop Diet
Lose weight and credibility

This is an exclusively digital diet and the results can only be seen online. Using the PhotoShop diet you can lose many kilograms in minutes and have the chiseled features of a top model for your Facebook profile pic. It involves no calorie restriction whatsoever, although you can expect to get a double-take when people see your double chin in the flesh. With a lot more flesh than they were expecting.

Dieting Mantras

The power of positive affirmation

A dieting mantra is one of the many tools you can employ to stick to your weight loss plan. Using a positive affirmation can banish some of the negative thoughts that you may have and replaces them with nothing but glowing, wholesome positivity. Mantras can work for you because they help change your way of thinking and give you a positive mind-set. And they work in so many ways.

Try these, they're bound to help

These keep you sailing on the right course when temptation tries to wreck the navigation and steer you off course onto the rocky shores of Greggs bakery for a job lot of custard doughnuts and iced finger buns. Let the joy of these positive thoughts seep into your soul.

"I'm not as fat and unsightly as I was yesterday."

"Normal-sized clothes will fit me soon."

"I won't be an embarrassment to my children
for much longer."

"The laughter is about to stop."

"Structural reinforcement of my home
is a thing of the past."

"Things are going to stop wobbling from now on."

Get on top of your cognitives!

Dieting mantras can help counter what psychiatrists and children studying GCSE Psychology call a 'cognitive challenge'. Cognitive psychology believes that many of our problems and hang-ups are caused by us latching onto ideas and beliefs that are simply not true. Such as the moon is made of cheese. It's not. In other words – sometimes we can be our own worst enemy. (Even though most of the time we strive to be our own special friend.)

When a little voice says: "I'm hungry, I can't stand being so hungry," counter that little voice with: "There are millions of people in the world starving who won't get the chance to eat tonight. Suck on that fact chubby chops." You can bear to be hungry, you can see it through, get your pudgy fingers off the biscuit jar."

The 10-mantra path

Here are some great mantras that will help you lose weight:

> **"I feel great and I look great and everything's going to be great."**

> **"My clothes fit beautifully and I look fantastic."**

> **"I can easily resist temptation and stick to my diet."**

> **"My body is a temple. And I will get my worshippers!"**

> **"Nothing tastes as good as thin feels. Apart from bacon, obviously."**

> **"People are noticing the new me. I'm sweating less."**

> **"My best friend is fatter than me now."**

"My new shape is going to turn heads. This time for all the right reasons."

"I am throwing away my old jeans and buying a smaller size. Soon."

"My parking space outside 'Mr Chips' has been given to someone else."

It's All Milky Way's Fault

Snackistan

It's not the rise of McDonalds and Burger King or the evil corn syrup that is heaped into so much of today's processed foods that are the original villains of the piece. The blame for our snacking culture and the record levels of obesity in this country can be put down to the Milky Way. In the 1960s the chocolate bar was advertised as "the sweet you can eat between meals without ruining your appetite". That advertising message was imperative because food was so god-awful in the 1960s and 1970s that you needed a long run-up to make sure you could eat it. Along came the Milky Way and all of a sudden intra-meal snacking got a foot in the door. After Milky Way wedged it open, in popped a finger of Fudge, the

Double Decker, the Caramel Wafer, Tunnock's Teacake and the Viscount biscuit – and all hell was let loose. Tunnock's may have been producing fine biscuitry since 1890 but it was the TV sell of the Milky Way lifestyle that unleashed snackmageddon on us. The more calorific Mars bar helped you work, rest and play – the work and play bit was a given, but the rest…?

A life-size diet aid

Fat photos can be a big motivation to lose weight. A big incentive to shed some pounds is to stick some embarrassingly fat photos of yourself on the fridge, on your computer and on the toilet door – maybe stick some up at home, too. Another good way would be to get a fat cut-out of yourself. It shouldn't only be Slimmer of the Year who gets to have a lifesize cut-out of their fat former selves to show how good they've been. (There are only two variants to the Star Slimmer photo opportunity. The first is wearing a set of the pre-diet trousers and holding the waist out. The second is standing looking pleased next to your fat cut-out. Everyone always has a better haircut than their cut-out.) That way you can have a ready comparison of how well you're doing.

In the future, when we have 9 billion people on the planet and the cost or lack of food is causing serious social unrest, fat people in guilt-ridden Western society will become even more stigmatised than they are now. The greedy, piggy-eyed, pudgie-fingered fatsos will need to be given a BMI target. Broach a certain predetermined live weight and the fatty in question should be made to walk round with a fat cut-out of themselves. It'll be like criminal electronic tagging, but instead of wearing a small ankle bracelet, they'd have a fat twin. They say laughter is the best medicine and it would certainly be recompense for those of us not draining grain silos.

10 things dieters don't want to hear

"What do you need to lose weight for?"

"Yes, you really need to lose weight."

"I can eat anything I like and I never put on an ounce."

"No, those are 120 calories EACH."

"Oh go on, it won't hurt to have a cheeky little…"

"There's no point in dieting, you'll only put it all back on."

"Why don't you get a head start with a bit of liposuction?"

"Won't it alter the perspective on all your belly tattoos…?"

"Now I know why you're looking so pasty."

"I've signed you and Mimi up for the blueberry pie-eating contest."

10 Answers to the statement: 'You don't need to lose weight…'

"So, did you want me to die of a heart attack…?"

"Yeah…? Chubby Chaser!"

"That's very kind of you to say, but you DO need to go to SpecSavers"

"Would you like me to get naked and point out the flaws in your argument?"

"Dieting is the new rock'n'roll – well, just the rock actually."

"You're only saying that because you want me to stay as overweight as you."

"All my transvestite clothes shrunk in the tumble
dryer and they are so-o-o-o-o expensive."

" I'm only doing it to lower my large partner's
self-esteem."

You're right, I am mentally challenged – thanks for
pointing it out."

"You do."

The most farcical bit of diet advice you can get

If you have a 'baloney filter' that takes out all the crass
and incredible statements you read on dieting websites,
then trust me, you'll be changing the filter very often. You
will have to read advice written by practicing
'Naturopaths'. Putting aside the initial reaction that this
is a pedestrian route to a nudist beach, the naturopath
will talk about lifestyle and diet and becoming a
flexitarian.

A flexitarian is a semi-vegetarian, someone who likes to
eat a mostly vegetable diet but cannot resist the lure of
the bacon sandwich. As Al Murray's pub landlord says,
the bacon sandwich has unique restorative powers and

should be grouped in with goji berries, spirulina algae and blueberries as a superfood.

Naturopaths seldom want you to 'diet', because dieting is seen as a skittish, lightweight thing. They're much too deep to recommend you a diet. No, they want to empower you to **change your relationship with food**. In fact, they will probably urge you to have a conversation with yourself about this. My relationship with food is for the most part fleeting. When it gets beyond the sell-by date it's history, there's no sentimentality involved. True, my wife will remind me of things she found in my fridge when she first met me that seemed like they'd developed a life of their own, but there was no relationship involved, I'd simply forgotten they were there.

Someone who *did* have a relationship with his food is the arch villain Hannibal Lecter, but it was very one-sided. *The Silence of the Lambs* protagonist would have made a really interesting guest on *Come Dine With Me*. He would have to be the last one on, of course, and everybody would run screaming when he brought out the fava beans and his bottle of fine chianti. And they'd have to rename the series, *Come Dine On Me*.

Another thing that naturopaths like to say is 'listen to your body – it instinctively knows what is best for it'. Baloney. My body is always telling me to go down to the pub and stop in for a kebab on the way back, but my head says no. My head says that it will increase my waistline and give me a headache the morning after. My wallet occasionally joins in the argument and backs up my head to the extent that my body feels like it's being marginalised. At which point my wallet will probably make an inappropriate joke, like it would have to be a pretty big margin for your body to fit in and it'll all kick off. It ends when my head insists that it is the one that's driving so everyone else shut up.

In 2011 the figure for obesity among adults was 25% in England and 27% in Scotland. A quarter of the population are being told by their body that it's okay to have the extra pie and that the iced Danish from the petrol station cashdesk is a good idea. Our bodies don't instinctively know what is best for us, they need to be told.

And talking about rubbish advice...

One of the previous books in the Grumpy series – *The Grumpy Git's Guide To Technology* – tackled the irritating things on the Internet, in particular the kind of adverts that deserve some form of capital punishment for the perpetrators. You know the ones, you see them all the time on low-rent websites – "Cut down a bit of belly fat every day by never eating these five foods" … says London mom who earns $900 a week from home … and recommends you cover a 50-year-old woman's face with Clingfilm.

These five foods can be anything from Macaroons to Monster Munch or Walnuts to White Chocolate, it really doesn't matter. The most important thing is – don't click the flipping link, it only encourages them. What helps you lose weight is a lack of calories. Look at a calorie counter and work it out.

Diets We Know Don't Work

Dare to dream

Cynics say that most diets don't work and that sooner or later you're going to pile everything you lost back on again. And it could be worse even; you might put back on more than you started with. Diet detractors love to cite examples of people who've ballooned their way up and down the bathroom scales, but that's missing the point. Fearless TV investigator Jacques Peretti (whose name sounds like Hercule Poirot, but whose voice sounds like Stephen Merchant and Ian Holloway) poked his nose into the dieting business to point out what a bunch of charlatans run it. He found out that diet firms cannot guarantee that people will lose weight forever. It's a sensational claim but one he stuck with. Jacques found that most people who invest in long-term diets put all the

131

weight they lost back on again, which Jacques thinks is a great big con. The point he missed about diets is that they give people the opportunity to lose weight and the feeling they are in control and can lose weight if they put their mind to it. Many like the idea, try it, stick with it for a while, then decide it's not for them.

That's the difference between a diet and a tattoo – you're stuck with a tattoo. All the time diets are working and people are saying nice things, diets are good and the perfect morale boost. Why they've even helped WeightWatchers Ambassador Patsy Kensit get her sparkle back – after four marriages and a faded pop career she says "the best is yet to come" and you've got to respect that kind of plucky optimism.

The Lance Armstrong Diet

This is a diet where you pretend to be on a diet, then deny having eaten stuff. On the Lance Armstrong Diet you eat exactly what you did before, but do it in a private place, like your hotel room, where nobody can see you. If people challenge you, and say "you're not actually on a diet are you?" you get furious with them and respond with "I'll see you in court, buddy!".

The Chives-Free Diet

My mother-in-law has a great diet which she's explained to me at length. When I woke up she was still going. She listed all the things she was allowed to eat, which sounded like just about everything. In fact the only thing I didn't notice on the long list was chives, making it the Chives-Free diet. She says it suits the way she lives and I can see why. It hasn't made a discernible difference to her figure, whenever she comes round to our house she still shades most of the drive and you can hear the paving slabs audibly wince.

The Samoan Diet

Limit yourself to just 5,000 calories a day by cutting out the box of After Eight mints and the half pint of Baileys. At both lunch and dinner.

The Victorian Diet

An old-fashioned slimming device advertised in the late Victorian period was the tapeworm. This was often employed as a last resort by young ladies to get their waists to the impossibly slim dimensions that fashion demanded. It was the *Six Weeks to OMG* of the last century, but once started it wasn't as easy to give up –

once the tenacious blighters got a hold of the intestines they liked to hang on. However, there were other diets doing the rounds at the time based on very little science and much conjecture, including one we've dubbed...

Six Weeks to Oh Good Lord
Breakfast: Half a dozen oysters with lemon and plenty of Darjeeling or Ceylon tea.
Morning tea or 'Elevenses': A lemon-cheese tart and a cup of Congou or Imperial tea.
Luncheon: Lightly poached haddock with boiled new potatoes.
Low tea: Plenty of Pekoe or Souchong tea with a Scottish Scone.
High tea: Brown Windsor soup and a bread roll plus a cup of Gunpowder tea or lemonade.
Dinner: Roast fowl with two vegetables of choice, followed by Plum Duff, no custard.
Supper: Pineapple water ice.

A Victorian visionary

Continuing the Victorian theme, many people remember the adverts with the late Brian Glover voice-over for Allinson's bread "wi now't taken out". Dr Thomas Allinson was more than a purveyor of wholemeal bread, but his dietary advice was shunned for years. Born in Hulme, Manchester, he trained as a doctor in Edinburgh and went on to challenge the medical system of the day by heavily criticising the use of opiates, mercury and arsenic, commonplace at the time. He was a fervent supporter of women's rights and his *Book For Married Women*, which gave advice on how a woman could exercise birth control and not be subject to successive pregnancies 'more than her constitution will bear' was banned. Allinson was prosecuted by magistrates for producing a pamphlet "that contained as much filth as could be compressed into a given space".

He had already been struck off the medical register in 1892 after accusing most doctors of "being in the ranks of professional poisoners". Something the general medical council of the time didn't take a kindly, liberal view upon. Above all his campaigns Allinson was a passionate believer in healthy living and the benefits of wholemeal bread.

"I have not eaten any fish, flesh or fowl since February 1882, as I find I can do my work much better without these things. When I first started life for myself, I had only my earnings to fall back on and I found a non-flesh diet allowed me to make most of the little I had and what I earned. Now I find such a diet allows me to make the most out of my powers and so I keep to it…

"Let me feed people on brown bread, grain foods,

vegetables and plenty of fruit and I will make the people sober without a single temperance lecture and without an Act of Parliament. If people live properly, they will neither have a desire for strong liquor, nor will they take it…

"On this simple diet, which will not cost a shilling a day, I work fourteen hours out of the twenty-four. Am bright and merry at the end of the day, and have uninterrupted good health."

When the value of whole grain bread was firmly established during the First World War Allinson, who by then had started his own Natural Food Company, was invited to re-register as a doctor, but would have none of it. Many of his ideas on health are now mainstream and appear in modern dieting books. He believed in the value of cold baths – *Six Weeks to OMG* – and he was also a fan of fasting – *The Fast Diet*.

"A common sense old friend one day told me that he often did me out of a fee by taking a long walk and going without a meal, whenever he felt out of sorts. A man who lived to be 180 years old attributed his long life to the fact that he only ate one meal a day, took all his food cold and fasted the first and fifteenth of every month."

He wasn't good at guessing ages, though.

Timeline of extreme diets

How badly do you want to lose weight? Would you knowingly ingest a parasite to do the hard work for you? Agree to live on wine only? Or would you adapt the way you eat by swapping your cutlery around?

WINE ONLY
c. 1080 After the feasting days of the Romans it was famine and hard times all the way through the middle ages. Only the royals could afford to get fat, and William the Conqueror got so fat he couldn't sit on his horse. Thinking it was food that was adding to his great girth he switched to a wine-only diet and completely cut out the croissants and pain au chocolat. It didn't work. When King Philip of France insulted the Norman about his bulk it was war. While besieging Nantes 'Guillaume' was thrown hard against the pommel of his horse and died from the injury. They tried to put him into a stone coffin, but his diet had been so ineffective that he didn't fit.

MEAT FREE
1502 Venetian nobleman Luigi Cornaro's dissolute lifestyle allegedly brought him near the brink of death at the age of 35. He then decided to mend his ways and started on what was the very first low-calorie diet, allowing himself 400g of solid food every day and 500g of wine. After a while he decided that this was still a bit gluttonous and cut all meat from his diet; the only animal

protein he relied on was an egg. He wrote his first dieting blockbuster at the age of 83 and followed this up with three further versions at 86, 91 and 95. This surely makes him the patron saint of 5:2. He published the work under his own name and not 'Venice A. Nobleman'.

THE 'AVOID SWAMPS' DIET

1727 Thomas Short M.D. in his treatise *Discourse on the Causes and Effects of Corpulence* of 1727 noticed that the majority of corpulent people he encountered came from low-lying swamps and so to avoid getting fat you needed to move to higher, drier ground. This innovative theory might have come from original research, but he could simply have noticed that Peter Paul Rubens liked to paint plumply voluptuous women and he came from the low countries. Rubens gave us the term Rubenesque. Today Rubenesque women are sometimes known as BBWs – Big Beautiful Women.

CUTTING OUT LUST

1829 Sylvester Graham was the seventeenth child of a Connecticut clergyman and was himself ordinated as a Presbyterian minister. He railed against the evils of white bread and masturbation, proselytizing the cause of wholemeal, and indeed may have been the inspiration for British wholegrain evangelist Thomas Allinson. Graham invented the Graham Cracker because he thought food should be bland and not cause excitement, which was unhealthy. He also didn't think people should eat while their emotions were high and that animal byproducts created lust in the human psyche. The Graham Diet, largely vegetarian, was aimed at ridding people of impure thoughts. American puritans loved it, especially the Kelloggs.

"I'M ON A BANT"

1863 William Banting was a formerly obese London undertaker who asked his doctor for advice to lose weight. The low-carbohydrate diet he was recommended was originally intended to curb diabetes, but it transformed Banting's life and he lost 50lb. It was very similar to the subsequent Atkins diet, but in Victorian London it was viewed as extreme and he was vilified for suggesting you cut out sugar, starch, beer, milk and butter. Banting lived till 83 (unlike the perpetually unlusty Sylvester Graham who expired at 57) and his surname became the verb for dieting.

THE TAPEWORM

1890s The fashion for extraordinarily thin waistlines in the Victorian era led to extreme measures. The first cases of anorexia cropped up and the Tapeworm Diet reared its ugly parasitic head. Dieters would swallow beef tapeworm cysts in the form of a pill and the worms would develop in the intestine parasitising the body of food and nutrients and calories. Once the weight had been lost, the dieter would take medicine designed to kill the tapeworm and hope that it wasn't too much fuss getting it out the other end. Oh and that they didn't cause blindness, epilepsy or liver failure.

CHEW CHEW

1903 The Fletcherize Process. Horace Fletcher was a fat San Francisco art dealer, who liked to chew things over. He came up with the idea that if you chewed food 32 times you could absorb any nutrients that were contained in it and could spit out the rest. It didn't make for great dinner parties but he lost weight because he wasn't taking in calories. John Harvey Kellogg thought it was a great idea and encouraged visitors to his sanatorium to Fletcherize. Throughout the world legions of small children follow Fletcher and spit out Kelloggs products – not for any reason, just because they can.

'REACH FOR A LUCKY'

1928 'The modern way to diet!' Long before the *Madmen* era, Lucky Strike cigarettes in the States thought that they could make their product more attractive to women by advertising it as a diet aid. 'To maintain a slender figure, no one can deny the truth of the advice: Reach for a Lucky instead of a sweet.' They paid money to film stars and celebs to vouch for this advice. Lady Grace Drummond-Hay, the first woman to travel around the world by air in a Zeppelin cut a glamorous figure and proclaimed in an advert: "I have practiced this for years and find it a most effective way of retaining a trim figure."

MEAT ONLY
1920s Canadian explorer Vilhjalmur Stefansson, lived with the Inuit in the Arctic circle from 1906–1907 and came back with the Inuit Diet – the first No Carbohydrate diet. He demonstrated that you could live healthily on 90% meat and fish as the Inuit did for six to nine months of the year. A lack of oven-ready penguins made the diet almost impossible to follow.

DRINKING MAN'S DIET
1964 Robert Cameron published the 48-page *Drinking Man's Diet* and sold 2.4 million copies. At the time everyone wanted to be Dean Martin so it made sense. It was really just a bog standard low-carb diet that included a few drinks. It also appealed to men because it was only 48 pages long.

THE AIR DIET
1970s Breatharianism is a radical new age idea. Breatharians can live without food and drink, and subsist only off "pranic light". According to practitioners, pranic light is a channelled form of the sun's rays. Another more common term for it is starving.

ELTON'S GLASSES
1980s The Vision Dieter was a pair of blue sunglasses that were designed to make food look less appealing so you wouldn't eat so much. Right.

EAR TOUCHING
1980s Ear Staples. A small staple inserted across the outside of the inner ear is supposed to suppress your appetite – a little like acupuncture. When you felt hungry the idea was to touch the staple and then the feeling of hunger would disappear. Presumably if someone's gone to the trouble of inserting a piece of metal into a sensitive part of your body you feel obliged to lose weight and make the procedure worthwhile. This is still more effective than diet soaps containing seaweed with active ingredients that penetrate the skin and break down both fat and cellulite...while tightening and firming and giving you a slight glowing tan, etc. etc.

COTTON WOOL BALLS
1980s The Cotton Wool Ball Diet – yes, you've guessed it, you swallow wet cotton wool balls to make yourself fuller before you eat. Genius. It's not known if they prove useful on the way out.

AS RECOMMENDED BY GOD
1990s The Hallelujah Diet is one of the few diets we know that's been dictated by the man upstairs. If you believe the diet's supporters it's God's will that we only eat foods

mentioned in the Bible, more specifically, Genesis, Chapter 1. These foods are all-natural, vegan foods. Mindful of energy prices, he only wants us to cook a small proportion of them, the majority should be eaten raw.

It's not his only work on diets, though. Who can forget his earlier seminal work, The Lent Diet, that involved fasting for 40 days and 40 nights. The bit about going off into the wilderness wasn't particularly easy to follow, but one man's wilderness is another man's larder (see The Tramp's Diet, p. 116).

LOVE IT LIGHT

2005 The Diet Coke and Cigarette Diet was definitely a case of history repeating itself, with the return of 'Reach for a Lucky', although this time round it was taken up by college girls in the States who used it to lose weight to fit into prom dresses. Less of a diet and more of an OMG panic that they weren't going to look good on the dancefloor – more Ann Widdecombe than Ola Jordan.

TINY FORKS

2011 You're forked! Star of BBC series *The Apprentice*, Lord Alan Sugar has devised a diet – or more specifically, a method of eating – which certainly keeps the pounds off as far as he's concerned. Instead of using the normal-sized fork supplied by restaurants he has his own special accoutrements.

When he goes for one of his many business meals he's obliged to attend, instead of using the normal-sized fork supplied by the restaurant, he whips out his own mini fork. It takes him so much longer to eat that he feels full before he's finished. It's a great system if you like people staring at you while you plough towards the end of what has become a very cold meal.

He really should go on *Dragon's Den* with Nick Hewer and see if he can get backing for a potential new Alan Sugar range: mini plates, mini cups, mini bowls and mini wine glasses. That would make great television, a cross between an investment programme and tag wrestling.

Homeopathic cheese pizza

There are some crafty ways that you can save calories without forgoing taste. Anybody who's bought a selection of low-calorie dressings will realise the brutal truth that some things should not exist in a low-calorie form. However there is a splendid way to enjoy a normal pizza with a generous cheese topping without breaking the calorie bank. Cook it like a normal pizza, but before the pizza is served, scrape all the cheese off and throw it in the bin. Pizza is a very receptive medium and will retain the memory of cheese. You get all the delicious cheesy taste of a mature cheddar cheese pizza, but with none of the calories – and none of the cheese!

Homeopathic light ale

Here's a great way to lose weight while you're down the pub. After you've downed a pint of light ale, leave a couple of drops in the bottom. Next, fill the glass back up to the top with tap water. This gives you the rich and satisfying taste of homeopathic light ale. Encourage all the drinkers in the group to indulge in a homeopathic version of their favourite tipple and watch the barman's face crease up with laughter and delight as he realises he can't collect your glasses yet.

Homeopathic café latte

Many of the recipes recommended by the diet plans allow for plenty of tea and coffee to keep us hydrated and feeling not-so-hungry. The typical stand-bys are always black coffee and herbal tea, which have very few calories indeed. But you can still get all the flavour of a latte with none of the added calories by drinking a homeopathic latte. This time we are not simply going to get you to add water to a few drops of your favourite drink, such as in homeopathic Red Bull, homeopathic vodka and homeopathic San Pellegrino.

Prepare or buy yourself a lovely café latte from your favourite coffee vendor and while you're doing it, buy a double espresso. Tip all of the café latte away, but leave a few drops in the bottom. Then transfer those two precious drops into the virtually calorie-free espresso. You'll find that the delicious café latte taste has transformed the espresso into homeopathic café latte. Voila! A treat indeed and none of the calories*. Works with sugar, too.

To save yourself some money, why not take a trip down to your local coffee shop with a friend and instead of tipping the café latte away, take two drops and then hand it to them.

* Don't be tempted to put more than two drops of café latte in as it might overwhelm the flavour.

'Vimto Waft'

When I put forward the concept of homeopathic light ale to my friend Nicola, her eyes shone brightly and she exclaimed "Vimto waft!" Her granny would get the last dregs in the bottle of Vimto and then fill it up with water to produce the elixir known as Vimto Waft. The classic fizzy fruit drink is still incredibly popular in the Middle East where a lot of it is drunk during Ramadan, so the potential for the further spread of Vimto Waft is huge.

Google
Calories

Make the most of food that is zero calories!

Those who are blighted by an addiction to golf will know that it has very strict rules. And like dieting, very occasionally you can turn a blind eye. In golf there is the 'mulligan' where an errant stroke can be played again, provided the game is being played for fun – mulligans can't be applied in The Open or the European PGA Championship. It's the same in dieting. Google calories are items of food that do not count to your average daily calorie total. They should have a kcal value, but no, they're a big fat zero.

The name Google Calories is derived from the popular website search engine. Although Google make millions of pounds from businesses in the UK, they pay very little tax to the Chancellor of the Exchequer because of their complex and wholly legitimate tax arrangements. Hence, they would seem to have a considerable tax burden and an obligation to the UK but no, they don't. So what you'd think would be a great big slug of calories, actually turns out to be nothing.

Here are a range of things that count as Google calories:

• Any food that is dropped on the floor.
• Any food that is left on someone else's plate after they've finished and walked away.
• Any food that is found down the back of the sofa – such as a Malteser with fluff on, or a reasonably un-stale Crawford's Cheddar.
• Any single food item that is stolen from someone else's plate, the most common item being a chip. Only a single chip counts, multiple chips will be charged at the standard rate.
• Any food that is passed to you in a romantic kiss by your loved one – this only tends to happen very early in the relationship.
• Any food found out on a walk – such as a blackberry or hazelnut, or a mushroom if you want to play Russian roulette with some of nature's most poisonous toxins.
• Any food that is stolen from an animal.
• Any flies you inadvertently swallow while cycling.
• Any food that you're asked to try as part of the cooking process to see if it is: too sweet/not salty enough/too sour/too spicy/not spicy enough/…going to make everyone nauseous.
• Any sample obtained as part of a supermarket tasting

session. These are potentially hilarious situations if you can fake a choking reaction.

• Baby food. Unless you're on the baby food diet, which is one of those diets where you have to question the person's sanity in eating 17 small meals a day consisting of manufactured baby meals, which despite the variety of labels, actually only taste of three different things. It's not surprising that you have to do the whole, "ooh look, there's a train going into the tunnel" routine when you taste what you're making your children eat.

Obviously you can't push this theory and just as mulligans are not a part of professional golf, you can't throw all your food on the floor and claim that it's no calories. Equally, you can't go and steal a steak off someone else's plate and say that it's no calories – this isn't *Tom and Jerry*.

There are some chancers who would like to push those boundaries even further and claim that broken biscuits are Google calories, but if you live with a clumsy partner whose food handling skills are not up to much, then you might tub out pretty quickly on packets of value custard creams tossed absent-mindedly into the biscuit tin. There's also another lobby that thinks Christmas Day shouldn't be included, but that's more like Google calendar than Google calories. It's the thin end of the wedge, too. Given that foot in the door it would soon be birthdays they were going to claim as an exclusion day, then partners' birthdays, close relations' birthdays and so it would go on. Soon they would add Boxing Day, New Year's Day, Easter and then the bank holidays.

A Lack of Calories...

I began to notice a shameless appetite again, a ravenous desire for food inside that grew steadily worse and worse. It gnawed without mercy in my chest, kept up a strange and silent labour in there. It was like a couple of dozen tiny creatures who put their heads over to one side and gnawed awhile, then put their heads over to the other side and gnawed awhile, lay for a moment absolutely still, started again, bored their way in without making noise or hurrying, and left behind them empty areas wherever they went.

(Knut Hamsun, *Hunger*, 1890)

Oh yeah, your body notices

One thing common to many diets is the effect on the body when you reduce the number of calories. Far from doing the British thing and carrying on regardless, pretending not to notice, your body is very upfront and American about this lack of input. When the body senses it's being short-changed in the calorie department it impacts on the brain and there are important cognitive changes. These are:

- Anxiety and an increased risk of depression
- Poor decision making skills
- A tendency to become irritable
- A tendency to be reactive
- The inability to concentrate
- A withdrawal from social activities
- A declining interest in sex
- A lack of enjoyment in previously enjoyed activities

All in all, the effects of starvation, even if they're not allied to your financial position, will make you as miserable as sin. Reading that list it's hard to see where the euphoria or the re-energising vibe of going without food comes from. In fact reading that list you can appreciate the phrase fat and happy and why people who live it large and are large are having such a good time.

Cronies

There is a group of pitifully thin Californians who are self-confessed CRONies – that's Calorie Restriction with Optimal Nutrition. They limit what they eat to around

152

1,500 to 1,900 calories a day – around 1,000 calories less than they should be having. Instead of having two or three meals, they split it up into around 10. To be absolutely certain that a typical breakfast of a mixture of kale, shallots, sprouted oats, tomato paste and olive oil (Yum) is just 170 calories, all the ingredients have to be carefully weighed. This sounds so much fun, it's surprising that there aren't more cronies out there.

The Xmas Party is no doubt a riotous affair, with them all kicking back and going crazy – forget the yard-of-ale, this lot probably go wild by challenging each other to drink a whole test tube of low-alcohol lager. Down in one!

Cronies are typical of many calorie restrictors who turn up on television to extol the virtues of what they're doing, but all they seem to do is exude an air of underlying fearfulness. The fear is that after all the care they're taking, something else in their genetic code is going to come out and bite them on the bum and all that self-sacrifice which they pass off as "second nature to me now" will be for nothing.

Losing your caloric virginity

One of the great sadnesses of dieting is that it forces you to lose your calorie innocence. You can no longer turn a blind eye to what is an extravagantly high calorie item, or ignore the benefits of a low-calorie replacement. Once you know that a slice of white bread is 140 calories, it's very hard to forget it. Occasionally products clamour for your attention by shouting on the packaging that they're only 90 kcal each! – which is not such a great selling point when you think that they look so unappealing that they should be about half of that. Driven to the shops for the mid-afternoon biscuit it's very easy to skip over the kind of crunch bar that would make only a squirrel's mouth water (or a Californian Cronie excited) and go for the KitKat, blissfully ignorant that four fingers of chocolate covered wafer could set you back 233 kcal.

Look up that information online and various websites will give you the calorie count for 'one serving' of KitKat. One serving! It's a flipping KitKat – you want to know if it's a two-finger or a four-finger Kit-Kat that's all, not what 'one serving' of it is.

Once inadvertently primed with this calorie knowledge, factoring it into a munchies-selection process only makes the choice harder and more drawn out. There's the cost to be taken into account, the amount of bang-for-your buck or ping-for-your-pound to consider – should you get the £1 pack of nine small flapjacks or the £1.50 double chocolate cookies? Add the calorie consideration into the process and you could go missing from your desk for half the afternoon.

Are you a member of the Caloric Stasi?

The notorious East German police, the Stasi, exacted a tight control over the population of the DDR until the late 1980s. Equally, there are many dieters who exert a tight control of what they allow onto their plate, based on calorific value. Both regimes know/knew that information is power. Test out if you would qualify as a high-ranking member of the Calorie Stasi by taking our test.

1.Which is more calorific?
a) Red wine
b) White wine

2. If you were offered 100g of lentils or 200g of pitted, drained black olives, which would have the most calories?
a) Olives
b) Lentils

3. Both of these items can have an overpowering effect on dinner guests, but which is more calories per 100g?
a) Red onion
b) Garlic

4. Goji Berries are regarded as a superfood by some –

what do you think their calorific value is per 100g?

a) 36

b) 312

5. Lard is a much better insult when conjoined with a part of the human anatomy than vegetable oil, but which has the most calories?

a) Lard

b) Vegetable oil

6. Which is more per 100g?

a) Frozen peas

b) Potatoes

7. Neither are going to turn you into the Incredible Bulk, but which has fewer calories?

a) Celery

b) Cucumber

8. In the showdown of least calorific fruits which comes out on top as the lowest per 100g?

a) Watermelon

b) Grapefruit

9. Whole milk is around 65 calories per 100ml – so how much is semi-skimmed milk?

a) 33

b) 50

10. It's not a regular quandary for pub goers – but which would you choose if you wanted least calories per 100ml?
a) Lager
b) Champagne

11. Pasta often tastes better with some grated Parmesan cheese – much better than it would with coconut flakes. But which is the most calorific?
a) Grated Parmesan
b) Coconut flakes

12. In this seafood tussle – which comes off as the calorie lightweight…?
a) Prawns
b) Mussels

13. How many calories are baked beans per 100g?
a) Around 90
b) Around 190

14. That red swimsuit has been around for years, but is 100g of Special K less calorific than 100g of porridge?
a) Yes
b) No

15. If a two-fingered KitKat is 107 calories – what do you think a four-fingered KitKat should be?
a) 214 calories
b) 233 calories

Answers:
1. a) Red wine
2. b) Lentils
3. b) Garlic
4. b) 312
5. a) Lard
6. a) Frozen peas
7. a) Celery
8. b) Grapefruit
9. b) 50
10. b) Champagne
11. b) Coconut flakes
12. a) Prawns
13. a) Around 90
14. b) No
15. b) 233 calories – there's a little bit of extra chocolate linking the two together, and also we told you the answer in the text above.

Score: Give yourself 10 points for a correct answer.

If you scored:
120–150 You are the kind of sharp-witted, eagle-eyed zealot that the organisation has been looking for. You can quote the difference between four varieties of cream in your sleep and you never knowingly pass up an opportunity to share interesting calorie facts. Parties swing when you're around.

80–110 You could probably make the lower ranks, but you really need to spend more time with your calorie counter.

0–70 You are not a member of the Calorie Stasi. In fact you scored about the same number of points as one of the ingredients listed above, had they been able to indicate answers with their antennae.

Acknowledgements

The author could not have written the book without help from friends and colleagues: Emily Preece-Morrison, Jonathan White, Dicken Goodwin, Fiona Holman, Polly Powell, Nicola Newman, Charlotte Selby, Judith Abrahams-Huxford, Merle James and Joanna Pink.

Also in this series:.
The Grumpy Golfer's Handbook

Misery and despair on the golf links, at the driving range and even at the crazy golf course.

The Grumpy Gardener's Handbook

Tales of rampant slugs, leaning fences, smelly bonfires, weaselly neighbours and where to stick a gnome!

The Grumpy Driver's Handbook

A Clarksonesque look at the perils of driving, such as roadside cameras, trips to the airport and seat warmers.

The Grumpy Git's Guide to Technology

Ivor rants about laptops, websites, twitter, mobiles, cameras, XBox and anything loved by the digital generation.